True Veil:

The Veils Collapse

In dedication to my daughter Lillian
Moore, stepson and stepdaughter Imran and
Fiza. Know you three are loved and always
wanting what is best for you three.

Table of Contents

Chapter One: A Strong Sense of Foreboding

As the story of creation goes, O'rivera was a lonely Goddess who sought more from the endless expanse of the Great Void that surrounded her. She took it upon herself to fill that void with beings she could love and who, in turn, would love her. When she began, her first creations were the Altraties—celestial beings shaped from her very essence. They were her children and her proudest creations. The Altraties, eager to please their mother, used their powers to create stars, and moons, and all the celestial bodies that floated through the Great Void. But their greatest achievement, however, was a singular celestial body that surpassed all others. This was a world they named in their mother's honor. **Orivera.**

With the creation of Orivera came the birth of two distinct races; Men and the Mythenians. Men were forged from fire and blood, while the Mythenians were born from the Altraties' magic intertwined with earthly matter. Despite their differences, O'rivera loved them all equally, delighting in the harmony they shared. This golden age became known as **the Era of Mythen**, a time when Men, Gods, and Mythenians lived as brethren, prospering under O'rivera's watchful eye.

Yet, this blissful era was not to last. Ka'rael, the firstborn of the Altraties, grew restless. Consumed by jealousy and hunger for power, he turned on his siblings, devouring them and stealing their divine essence. No one knows the true depth of his motives, but his betrayal ushered in monsters, death, and all the evils that plague the world. O'rivera, distraught by her eldest child's betrayal and the loss of her other children, faced an agonizing choice. To protect her beloved creations from the corruption spreading through Ka'rael, she made the ultimate sacrifice. She sealed herself and Ka'rael away behind a veil, a barrier that kept the darkness from consuming the world she so cherished. It was not an act of defeat but one of love— a mother's desperate attempt to shield her children's creations from annihilation. Now, however, that Holy Veil is under threat.

***

The Royal Castle was a colossal beauty, with balconies that gave anyone opportune to be upon them to gaze out and see the entirely of the Capital city, as well as the glorious walls miles away that secured it. But as Princess Oriana stood on the castle balcony, she could not see that beauty. The darkening skies above her eyes were fixed on, had swallowed all that serenity and replaced it with a glooming forebode. Her hands clutched her heart as unease churned within her. These were not rain clouds, it was not the season for that, nor were they gathered by the smokes of a fire. She felt the weight of an impending calamity more clearly now. It felt suffocating. "Something bad is going to happen," she murmured, her voice trembling. The chill in her bones confirmed it.

"My Princess," a familiar voice called softly. Rubella Wynter, the Court Mage, approached with a bow. She was perplexed to have been summoned to this secluded part of the castle in secret by a common maid, rather than the Princess' personal guard. And even more baffled to see That Princess was here with no aid or guard by her side, pale and shaken. It was a sight that deepened her concern. "What's wrong?"

Oriana turned to her friend; her eyes glassy with fear. "I had a vision," she admitted. Her voice was quiet, but the words carried the weight of dread. Rubella's frown deepened; she knew all too well the toll these visions took on the Princess. Oriana had been cursed with the gift of foresight but lacked the affinity for Mythen needed to control it.

"Come, let us return to your chambers," Rubella urged gently. "You should rest before we speak further."

Oriana shook her head, her expression grim. "No. My chambers are shrouded by death."

Rubella's eyes widened. "Why would you say such a thing? Is something going to happen in the castle?"

The Princess's voice wavered as she replied, "Something bad has already happened. We just can't see the signs yet."

Rubella's heart raced, her duty as Voice and guardian screaming out at her to do something. "We must warn the King and Queen!" she decided firmly, stepping forward. But Oriana grabbed her hands, halting her.

"I can't share what I saw," Oriana said, her voice cracking. "And even if I did, it wouldn't change what's already began. This castle is doomed, I know that much." Her grip tightened, and tears brimmed in her eyes. "But with you it's different, I do not know your fate, so I see hope in you."

"You're not making any sense my Princess."

"I want you to be safe." Oriana declared out rightly. It was the most selfish words she'd ever uttered to her younger friend, and it was a wish heavy with a frightful sincerity. Rubella stared at her, confusion and dread warring within her.

"What are you saying?"

Suddenly, Oriana pressed something into Rubella's hand. "You must leave the castle at once— No…" She backtracked. "That wouldn't be enough. The Castle, the Kingdom even… you must take your daughter and flee to the far Borders of

Man at once. Only then will you be safe, will this be safe."

Rubella looked down at the object now in her possession. Her eyes widening in recognition. It was a gem, but not just any gem. Its surface shimmered with colors that seemed to shift and swirl like a living thing. It radiated warmth and power, it was a piece of Orivera's heart.

"Princess what is this madness?" The words leaked out of Rubella's mouth in a sharp gasp. And for good reason. This relic was proof of the true lineage ordained to reign over Men in the Goddess' absence. It was a treasure so dear to the kingdom that so few people in the Castle's inner circle were even aware of its existence.

"Ensure this does not fall into the wrong hands. Swear it to me,"

"Princess, I can't," Rubella said, her voice shaking. "T-this is beyond me. It is madness—treasonous even! If we're caught—"

"Rubella, please," Oriana interrupted, her tears falling freely. "I have no choice. You must do this."

Rubella struggled to maintain her composure as Oriana stood before her, tears brimming in both their eyes. The Princess took a deep, trembling breath, as though bracing herself for what had to be done. Slowly, she straightened, the weight of her decision settling visibly on her shoulders. When she spoke, her voice was resolute, and an unmistakable power filled the air around them.

"As Oriana Elyndral, true heir to Orivera and chosen by the Goddess herself, I command you to go."

The words resonated like a sacred decree, carrying the force of Mythen itself. Rubella gasped

as the air seemed to hum with Orivera's essence,
her knees buckling under the weight of the
command. Her trembling hands pressed against the
cold stone floor as she looked up at Oriana, awe-
struck by the faint glow now surrounding the
Princess. It was the unmistakable sign of divine
favor— the Mythen of Orivera's rightful rulers
made manifest.

Rubella's tears spilled over as she whispered
hoarsely, "I swear… I will do as you ask."

Oriana's shoulders sagged slightly with relief,
though the light around her remained, casting her
in a soft, ethereal glow. For a fleeting moment, she
no longer seemed burdened by fear but by
something greater— something Rubella could only
describe as purpose.

"But…" Rubella muttered as though afraid to
speak, the effects of the Princess' royal authority

still lingering on her, "When I reach the border. Then what?"

"When you reach the border, you'll know what to do." She assured her as she stared down the hall before adding softly, 'May the Goddess guide you.'

Rubella rose shakily to her feet, clutching the gem tightly. All of this felt so overwhelming, but her promise quickly drove her to action. Her heart pounded as she made her way through the castle corridors, her cloak pulled tightly around her to shield her face. She couldn't shake the feeling of wrongness that clung to her. The Princess's command weighed heavily on her, not just because of its implications but because of the chill that now seemed to pervade the castle. It was as if an unseen evil had been lurking all along, and only now could she sense it.

Oriana had saved her once.

Rubella had been a slave, taken by savages who'd orphaned her at a tender age. The Prince Charon and his knights had saved her, and it was chance that made it so she found her way to the castle to serve as a maid. It was there Oriana discovered her Mythen affinity and insisted she be trained among the kingdom's best mages to serve alongside her personal guard. It was just a whim, a simple favor. No one could have known the orphan girl from a village that no longer existed would turn out to be one of the most talented Mages within the kingdom. Without the Princess's kindness, Rubella would never have seen the chance to rise from maid to her position as Court Mage. She owed Oriana everything, yet this… this felt like abandoning her.

Rubella's steps faltered as she approached the guards stationed at the castle gates. The gem, now nestled securely in her pocket, seemed to pulse with a life of its own. She thought of her daughter,

Dalia, likely still with her grandparents in the city. The thought of her husband's parents brought a pang of longing at the recollection of his absence. He was a Commander in the Imperial guard and had gone North with a small battalion to suppress a growing monster insurgency there. She prayed he was safe, wherever he was.

"Court Mage," one of the guards greeted her with a bow. "Is something amiss?"

Rubella forced a calm smile. "I have an errand to run in the city. I won't be long."

The guards nodded and allowed her to pass. Once she was outside the castle walls, Rubella pulled her hood lower and quickened her pace. Her thoughts raced as she made her way toward the stables where her horse awaited. The gem felt heavier with each step. In the wrong hands, it could spell disaster— and her hands didn't feel so right anymore.

As Rubella saddled her horse, she glanced back at the castle one last time. Praying that whatever tragedy the Princess had foreseen, wouldn't be so cruel as to destroy it all. Mounting the horse, she urged it into a gallop, the wind carrying her away from the only home she had ever known.

***

Therion Wynter stood under the ominous grey blanket of clouds, his eyes fixed on the heavens. The sky was so dark that the Holy Veil's faint shimmer was nearly invisible, a dull sheen obscured by the encroaching storm. A foreboding sense of dread coiled in his chest, whispering that something terrible was on the horizon. He pushed the thought aside, tightening his cloak against the chill as he approached the war tent. Inside, the weight of decisions far greater than weather awaited him.

The tent's interior was lit by the steady glow of lanterns, their warm light casting long shadows over maps and documents strewn across the central table. Two figures stood waiting, their presence as commanding as the banners that represented their armies. Therion entered, his golden fist and crown insignia of the Emperor's Hand visible on his cloak. While his force was not known for magic or mythical feats, they were celebrated for their fierce loyalty and unyielding resolve in defending the kingdom.

The first of the two commanders, Lord Commander Vaelrik Durnhart, turned to greet him with a slight nod. The emblem of a silver dragon coiled around a spear was emblazoned on his chest, marking him as the leader of the Dracoseekers. Vaelrik's army specialized in hunting and subduing dragons, a rare and dangerous calling. The man himself was a towering presence, his weathered face marked by the lines of countless battles. His steely gaze suggested both experience and caution.

Beside him stood Lady Commander Lysara Kaedryn, the leader of the Arcane Vanguard. Her banner bore the image of an intricately designed starburst, representing her army's diverse array of specialized forces: mages, alchemists, and battle enchanters. Where Vaelrik exuded grounded pragmatism, Lysara carried an aura of precision and ambition, her piercing green eyes scanning Therion with a mix of curiosity and appraisal.

Therion inclined his head respectfully to the others. Vaelrik wasted no time, gesturing to the captain of his scouts, who stepped forward with a report.

"My lords and lady," the captain began, his voice steady but tinged with unease. "Our scouts have confirmed the location of the monster horde.

They're camped within the Shadowed Vale, approximately two leagues northeast. Their numbers are estimated at three thousand strong. The host comprises goblins, hobgoblins, trolls, and dire wolves. However, there are no signs of human hostages."

Murmurs rippled through the room. Monster Marches— a rare but deadly phenomenon where various monster races united to wreak havoc— were always a threat. Yet something about this gathering struck an odd chord.

"Three thousand," Vaelrik repeated, his gravelly voice cutting through the noise. "A formidable force, but not enough to justify summoning our combined armies. Even if they aimed to raid a large settlement, this horde would be a fraction of what we've faced before."

Lysara's sharp voice followed. "And yet they march. Their coordination alone is troubling. Who or what unites them? It warrants caution." She turned to the scout. "Send more scouts to ensure we aren't missing anything. I always want eyes on their movements."

The scout saluted and exited, leaving the commanders to their deliberations. Vaelrik's expression darkened further. "We must strike before their numbers swell. The longer we delay, the greater the risk of their forces converging with others."

Lysara smirked faintly. "An argument I'm inclined to agree with. My Vanguard will lead the charge. Our mages can decimate their front lines before the melee even begins."

Therion observed the exchange silently. The tension in the air was palpable, each commander's priorities shaping their strategies. Vaelrik's pragmatic caution clashed subtly with Lysara's eagerness for decisive action— and perhaps, glory.

Lysara's gaze shifted to Therion, her expression softening slightly. "Commander Wynter, I'd like to hear your thoughts. This must be the Emperor's Hand's first joint subjugation, and yet you appear remarkably composed. What do you make of the situation?"

Therion met her gaze evenly, his voice calm and measured. "We have limited information, but what we do know favors us. Their numbers are manageable, and we hold the advantage of surprise. If we act swiftly, we can contain the threat before it escalates."

He pointed to the map on the table, tracing a path with his finger. "Surrounding their encampment and launching a coordinated attack will cut off any chance of retreat. A simultaneous strike from all sides will ensure their forces crumble before they can regroup."

Vaelrik nodded thoughtfully, his lined face betraying a hint of approval. "A sound strategy. We'll position the Dracoseekers on their northern flank. My men will hold the line."

Lysara's smile returned, more confident now. "The Vanguard will take the east. My mages will ensure their leaders are neutralized swiftly."

Vaelrik's voice carried the weight of finality as he addressed the gathered officers. "Prepare your forces. We march at sundown. Dismissed."

The commanders saluted and filed out of the tent, leaving Therion to his thoughts. As he stepped outside, the cool evening air greeted him. The storm clouds overhead seemed heavier now, their oppressive weight matching the unease growing in his chest.

Sir Garrish, Therion's right-hand man, approached with a questioning look. "What's the plan, Commander?"

Therion's expression remained unreadable as he replied. "We march at sundown. Surround the monsters while they sleep and destroy the March before it grows too large to contain."

Garrish's brow furrowed. "Do you truly think the March is large enough to warrant this much force? One of Vaelrik's scouts told me they counted no more than three thousand."

Therion's gaze hardened, his tone firm. "Follow orders, Sir Garrish. That is all that matters."

The knight's lips pressed into a thin line, but he nodded. "As you command." With a brief salute, he left to prepare the troops. Therion allowed himself a moment of reflection. 'Something's not right here.' He could feel it in the air.

***

The butterfly danced on the breeze, its iridescent wings shimmering with colors so vibrant they seemed to defy the gray canvas of the sky. Each delicate movement painted a fleeting stroke of brilliance against the shadowy backdrop, a moment of defiance against the gloom that hung over everything. Its flight was mesmerizing, weaving through the thick air as if the encroaching storm could not dampen its spirit.

Dalia stood in awe, her small hand outstretched, hoping to draw the butterfly closer. Her wide eyes reflected its beauty, her breath held as if even the softest exhale might scare it away. She took a tentative step forward, her feet brushing against the cobblestones of the bustling market square. The world around her faded into a blur of muted sounds and shapes; all she saw was her lustrous friend.

"Come here," she whispered, her voice barely audible over the distant rumble of thunder.

But the butterfly fluttered higher, hovering just out of reach. Dalia's heart raced with childish excitement, her hand trembling as she willed it to come closer.

"Look, Grandpa, the butterfly!" she called, her voice breaking the spell. She turned toward the warm, hearty laughter of her grandfather, who was chatting with the fishmonger. In that instant that she looked away, the butterfly was gone.

Galen glanced up from the fishmonger's stall, his weathered face breaking into a smile. His beard, streaked with gray, framed a face full of kindness and mirth. "A butterfly, you say?" he asked, humoring her with a brief glance at the sky before hoisting a wrapped bundle of fresh fish into his satchel.

"It was so pretty," Dalia insisted, her voice tinged with disappointment now that she'd realized it was gone. She lowered her hand, staring wistfully at the empty space where the butterfly had been. "And it was right there…"

"But now it's gone." She pouted.

He chuckled, a rich and warm sound that seemed to echo the kindness in his eyes. "Well, it's probably found some shelter. Rain's on its way," he said, hoisting the paper sack filled with fish and crabs. "Come on, little one. Your grandma's waiting, and I don't think she'll want to hear about us getting caught in the rain."

Dalia perked up at the mention of her grandmother, but the sight of the fish didn't escape her notice. "Crabs?" she asked, her voice tinged with curiosity and delight.

Her grandfather grinned. "Got a good deal on them. You just wait—your grandma will make them the way you like."

As they walked home, her grandfather carried her on his broad shoulder. Despite his seventy years, Therion's father, Eldrin, was still strong and sturdy. Years of service in the royal guard had left him with a robust frame and a disciplined posture. His greying hair was neatly combed back, and his square jaw bore the faintest hint of a shadow, though his blue eyes carried a gentleness that softened his otherwise commanding appearance.

When they arrived at the modest stone house, Dalia wriggled free and ran to the window. Inside, her grandmother stood by the counter, a seasoned hand deftly chopping vegetables. Light from the window played on her features, accentuating the warm smile that lit up her face as she saw them approach.

"Back so soon?" she teased, wiping her hands on her apron as she opened the door for them.

Eldrin laughed, holding up the sack triumphantly. "Longer than you thought, but it was worth it. Look what I got— crabs!"

"Crabs!" Dalia echoed, running to hug her grandmother's waist.

Her grandmother, Maren, was a petite woman with kind eyes and silvery hair pulled into a neat bun. Her laugh was soft and musical as she stroked Dalia's hair. "Well, I hope you brought enough for all of us."

"Of course," Eldrin replied, setting the sack on the counter.

Dalia was a bright child, and immediately moved to help her Grandma, but while she did she began recounting her story about the butterfly, her words tumbled over one another in excitement at how lustrous the creature was. "It was so pretty, Grandma! It was shiny, like jewels, and so close!

I've never seen anything like it. But Grandpa didn't see it. It was gone when he looked."

Maren tilted her head, her smile growing fond. "A butterfly like that? You might have seen a blessing, sweetheart."

Dalia's brow furrowed. "A blessing?"

Maren crouched to her level, her voice soft and conspiratorial. "When I was your age, I used to hear stories about the goddess O'Rivera. They said she would send blessings to good children. But they're special blessings— meant only for the one who sees them. No one else can."

Eldrin, leaning against the table, made a skeptical face. "Blessings, is it?"

Maren shot him a playful look before turning back to Dalia. "I'm sure it was a blessing, just for you."

At this, Eldrin straightened and flexed his shoulder with a chuckle. "A blessing, eh? Funny, have you seen a blessing love?"

Maren laughed as she picked up the fish and crabs, carrying them to the counter. "I have. It wasn't a butterfly, though. Mine was a stag. A magnificent, white stag. Its antlers reached so high, they seemed to touch the clouds."

Eldrin watched her closely, his weathered face softening as she spoke. "And what did this stag mean?" he asked, his voice gentle.

Maren smiled knowingly as she leaned over to kiss the top of his head. "I took one look at it, and I knew I'd find a big, strong man to take care of me."

Eldrin chuckled, shaking his head as he returned to his seat. "You've got quite the imagination."

"Oh, I don't know," Maren replied, her voice light with teasing. "That stag hasn't let me down yet."

Dalia giggled as she climbed onto a chair beside her grandfather, her earlier disappointment forgotten. "So my butterfly is good too?" she asked.

Maren turned, holding a knife in one hand as she looked at her granddaughter with a warm smile. "Oh, sweetheart, it couldn't be anything else."

Dalia beamed, hopping down from her chair. Maren laughed, handing her a small bowl of herbs. "Start with these. Just sprinkle them on the fish— lightly now."

Eldrin leaned back in his chair, his fingers curling around the handle of a worn mug of tea, the steam rising and coiling in the cool air. His weathered face softened as he watched his wife and granddaughter at work. Maren's gentle humming filled the small kitchen, weaving into the comforting rhythms of their home. Dalia, perched on a stool too tall for her small frame, worked diligently under her grandmother's guidance. Her little hands scattered herbs over the fish with a precision that made her brow furrow in concentration.

Eldrin chuckled softly. "You'll have her running the kitchen soon enough, Maren."

Maren glanced over her shoulder, her smile lined with years of quiet love and sharp wit. "If she keeps this up, she'll put me out of a job before she's grown."

Dalia beamed, her brown eyes sparkling. "Grandma says I'm a natural!"

"That you are, darling," Eldrin replied, raising his mug in mock toast. "The finest cook in the making this side of the valley."

Outside, the sky darkened, heavy clouds rolling in like waves over the hills. The first drops of rain pattered against the windows, their rhythm slow and steady at first, then quickening as the storm settled over the home. Maren's hum shifted into a soothing tune, her voice low and steady as though determined to keep the rain from unsettling the peace within the walls.

Eldrin closed his eyes for a moment, letting the warmth of the room seep into his bones. The fire crackled softly in the hearth, casting golden light over the rough-hewn walls and well-worn furniture. The smell of sizzling fish began to waft through the air, mingling with the earthy scent of rain. The familiar comfort of it all made Eldrin's chest ache with quiet gratitude.

The steady chop of Maren's knife against the cutting board blended with the sounds of the rain, creating a rhythm that felt as timeless as the house itself. Dalia's chatter filled the spaces between, her voice bright and eager as she asked questions about the herbs, the fish, and the storm.

"Do you think the rain will last all night, Grandma?" Dalia asked, craning her neck to peer out the fogged-up window.

"Hard to say, love," Maren replied, her hands moving deftly as she sliced through a bundle of parsley. "But rain's good for the crops, even if it makes the roads muddy."

Eldrin opened his mouth to comment, but a sudden sound cut through the cozy din of the kitchen—a sharp, unexpected clatter. Hoof beats.

The rhythm was unmistakable, their rapid pace echoing faintly even through the steady drumming of the rain. Eldrin stiffened in his chair, his eyes narrowing. Maren paused mid-slice, the knife poised above the cutting board, her hum dying on her lips.

Dalia turned toward the door, her curiosity plain on her face. "Grandpa, is someone here?"

Eldrin stood slowly, his chair scraping against the floor. "Stay here," he murmured, his voice low. His movements were deliberate as he crossed to the door, his shoulders squaring as if bracing for whatever waited outside.

When he pulled the door open, the sight that greeted him made him pause. A chestnut horse stood in the rain-soaked yard, its sides heaving as though it had been ridden hard. On its back sat a familiar figure, drenched from head to toe.

"Rubelle?" Eldrin called, his deep voice carrying over the storm. "What in the world—?"

Rubelle dismounted quickly, pulling her cloak tighter around her. The expression on her face—tight-lipped, wary—sent a prickle of unease through him.

"Well, now," he said, stepping aside to let her in, "this is a surprise."

Maren stepped closer, her sharp eyes narrowing on the horse outside. "Rubelle, whose horse is that? We don't own one."

Rubelle hesitated, brushing rainwater from her cloak. Her hands trembled slightly, though she quickly tucked them under the fabric. Forcing a smile, she replied lightly, "Oh, just borrowed it for an errand. Nothing to worry about."

She stepped into the warm kitchen, her boots leaving muddy prints on the floor. Dalia ran to her, hugging her waist. "Mama, you're back!"

"Yes, sweetheart," Rubelle said, her voice softening as she stroked her daughter's hair. She glanced at the packed kitchen, the meal half-prepared, and took a breath. "Actually, Dalia, I need you to pack a few things. We're going on a little trip."

Dalia blinked up at her, confused. "A trip? Where?"

Rubelle's smile wavered, but she quickly recovered. "I'll explain soon. Just pack some clothes and your favorite toys, alright?"

The girl hesitated, looking toward her grandmother as if for permission.

Maren smiled gently, wiping her hands. "Go on, darling. I can finish up here. You'll have plenty of time to help me another day."

Dalia nodded, though her expression remained puzzled, and hurried off to her room.

The moment she disappeared, the lightness in Rubelle's demeanor crumbled. She exhaled shakily and slumped into a chair, gripping the edge of the table. "I'm sorry," she said softly, her voice thick with emotion. "I don't even know how to begin explaining."

Eldrin closed the door, his face serious as he returned to the table. "Then start from the beginning. What's going on, Rubelle?"

Rubelle swallowed hard, her fingers clutching at the damp fabric of her cloak. "I don't know everything," she admitted. "But I was commanded by the princess herself— she told me to take Dalia and leave the kingdom. Immediately."

Both Eldrin and Maren exchanged a long look. Rubelle braced herself for protests, for disbelief, but to her surprise, neither raised their voice nor argued.

Eldrin's brow furrowed as he rubbed his chin thoughtfully. "The princess wouldn't give such a command lightly," he said finally.

Maren stepped away from the counter, her calm demeanor steadying the air. "And you're certain it was the princess herself?"

Rubelle nodded. "Yes. She came to me directly. I... I can't explain it, but I felt her urgency. Something's happening. Something dangerous. I don't know what it is, but it's serious enough that she used her *authority* upon me."

Her voice cracked on the last words, and she bit her lip, tears welling in her eyes. "I don't want to leave you. I can't just—"

Maren interrupted her gently, placing a hand on her shoulder. "You have your orders, dear. We'll be alright here."

Rubelle stared at her, stunned. "You're not... upset? Or planning to come with us?"

Maren smiled faintly and shook her head. "If the princess didn't instruct us to follow, then we'd only slow you down. The fastest way to ensure your safety— and Dalia's— is to obey."

Eldrin grunted in agreement, though his eyes softened. "The princess knows what she's doing. If she said to leave, there's no time to waste second-guessing."

Rubelle stared at them, her mouth slightly open. "How can you both be so calm about this? I'm terrified."

Maren's expression grew tender as she leaned down, cupping Rubelle's face. "Because we've been through storms before, child. This may seem impossible now, but things have a way of righting themselves. You'll come back to us—when it's safe."

Eldrin reached out, patting Rubelle's hand. "You've got a good head on your shoulders. Trust it. And trust the princess. You'll see this through, and we'll still be here when you do."

Tears spilled from Rubelle's eyes as she nodded, overwhelmed by their steady resolve. She opened her mouth to speak, but a small voice interrupted her.

"I packed my bag, Mama!"

Dalia stood in the doorway, clutching a small satchel. Her face lit up with excitement. "Where are we going?"

Rubelle quickly wiped her tears and smiled, forcing a playful tone. "That's a surprise, sweetheart. But we'll have fun, I promise."

She stood, straightening her cloak and scooping Dalia into her arms. Turning back to her in-laws, she hesitated, searching for the right words.

"Thank you," she said finally, her voice barely above a whisper.

Maren hugged her tightly. "Go on now. You've got a journey ahead of you."

Eldrin gave her a reassuring nod. "Take care of her. And yourself."

With one last lingering look at the warm kitchen and the comforting faces of her in-laws, Rubelle turned and carried Dalia out into the rain. The door closed softly behind them, leaving only the sound of the rain tapping against the windows.

Chapter Two: The Hell Spawn.

Therion Wynter crouched low, his gloved fingers brushing the hilt of his sword. The dense thickets surrounding the clearing muffled the guttural growls and snarls of the monsters prowling ahead. Above, grey clouds churned ominously, casting a heavy shadow over the forest. Even the faint shimmer of the Holy Veil seemed subdued, as though the land itself recoiled from the horrors unfolding.

Therion's sharp, ice-blue eyes scanned the chaotic yet oddly coordinated movements in the clearing. Goblins darted about, their crude weapons clinking together as they barked guttural orders. Direwolves, their matted fur streaked with dried blood, prowled the outer perimeter, their glowing eyes flicking toward every shadow. At the heart of the horde, a crooked Troll loomed. Its hulking frame was sheathed in mismatched armor, and a massive, blood-stained cleaver rested casually on its shoulder, as though it weighed nothing.

"Think that's the leader?" Garrish whispered, his voice steady despite the tension in his posture.

Therion tilted his head slightly, never taking his eyes off the Troll. "Perhaps," he murmured, his tone edged with doubt. The strongest monster present was always the leader of the March, but it was also for that reason that they rarely left themselves so exposed. 'Is there's something else at play here.'

Garrish frowned, his hand tightening on the hilt of his sword as he noticed the look on his old friend's face. "You think there might be another leader in hiding?"

"No… not that." He shook his head, "It wouldn't make a difference if there were. We're here to slay them all."

Garrish nodded as they both noticed a brief flare of golden light flickered on a distant ridge to the east. Commander Lysara's battalion, the Silver Vanguard, was in position. Her disciplined troops held their ground, waiting for the final signal. On the western slope, Commander Vaelrik led his Crimson Templars to their own position, their blood-red banners rippling in the wind as his elite archers prepared to rain death upon the monsters below.

Therion's jaw tightened as he considered the weight of what was about to unfold. No matter how skilled a man was, when it came to dealing with monsters there was no certainty.

"Ensure our men are ready," he instructed Garrish. The captain nodded and slipped back into the ranks, where the clinking of armor and the low murmurs of warriors awaiting battle filled the air. The sky above rumbled, thunder crawling across the heavens like a prowling beast. A cold knot of foreboding settled deep in Therion's gut. They were all finally in position, awaiting the battle.

Moments later, the final signal blazed to life— a fiery explosion erupted from Lysara's mages, the shockwave rippling through the clearing. The goblins screeched in panic as flames devoured the edge of their camp. Direwolves yelped and scattered, their fur alight. Before the chaos could settle, Vaelrik's archers unleashed a precise volley, their arrows piercing through monsters with deadly accuracy. In an instant more than a third of the monster's forces perished, with their troll forces' especially depleted thanks to how their large builds made easy targets of them.

When the surviving monsters began to regroup, charging for the hills where the arrows came from, Therion knew it was time for him and his men to begin their assault. Therion's voice rang out, cutting through the cacophony. "Charge!"

The Emperor's Hand surged forward, their golden fist-and-crown banners trailing behind them like rays of sunlight piercing the gloom. Steel clashed against crude iron as goblins fell in droves. Wolves leaped, their snarls cut short by spears and blades. The air grew thick with the acrid stench of burning flesh and the metallic tang of blood. The Hobgoblins put up a bit of a fight, but there were no match for trained soldiers, especially without the aid of their larger defendants. Or so Therion thought.

A blood curdling cry rang out as Therion realized not all the Trolls had fallen.

Amid the chaos, Therion's focus remained locked on the lone surviving Troll. The hulking creature he'd noted prior clad in its shay armor roared, swinging its cleaver in a wide arc that sent a cluster of his men sprawling. He glared, now acknowledging that this was indeed the leader of the March. That made things simpler. The easiest way to thwart a monster March, was to slay their leader. Therion darted through the melee, his movements precise and deliberate as he closed in on the beast.

The Troll's glowing yellow eyes locked onto Therion, radiating a primal fury. It let out a guttural roar that echoed through the battlefield, raising its massive cleaver high above its head. The weapon, jagged and stained from countless battles, seemed as though it could cleave through steel and stone alike.

With a thunderous swing, the cleaver descended, aiming to crush Therion where he stood. He sidestepped just in time, the blade slamming into the earth with such force that the ground shook violently. Shards of rock and dirt exploded into the air, momentarily obscuring the beast. Seizing the opening, Therion pivoted and slashed his sword across the Troll's thigh. The steel bit deep into the thick, leathery skin, drawing a torrent of dark, viscous blood.

The Troll roared in agony, staggering but refusing to fall. Its massive fist lashed out in a sweeping arc. Therion leapt backward, narrowly avoiding a blow that would have crushed his ribs. The sheer power of the strike sent a gust of air rushing past him, a stark reminder of the monstrous strength he faced. Had it been anyone else, they would have been broken by such force.

Therion shifted his stance, circling the creature with measured precision. The Troll snarled, yanking its cleaver free from the ground and swinging it in a wide, brutal arc. Therion raised his shield, bracing himself as the blade collided with it. The impact was catastrophic—his shield buckled under the strain before shattering completely, shards of metal and wood flying in all directions. The force of the blow drove him back several paces, his arm screaming in pain from the impact.

Only his honed reflexes and disciplined training kept him standing. *Had it been anyone else...* he thought grimly, shaking the numbness from his shield arm. The Troll's size made it slow, but every blow it delivered was like a battering ram. Even a single mistake could prove fatal.

The beast lunged again, this time with a vicious overhead swing. Therion sidestepped once more, his boots skidding slightly on the blood-soaked ground. He retaliated with a sharp strike to the Troll's knee, his blade cutting through tendon and bone. The creature howled, its leg buckling beneath it as it fell with a deafening crash.

But before Therion could deliver a finishing blow, the air grew heavy with an unnatural energy. The Troll's guttural voice began to chant, its tone low and reverberating with a sinister cadence. The words it spoke were harsh and alien, vibrating with a palpable darkness that made the hairs on the back of Therion's neck stand on end.

His heart pounded. Monsters didn't use magic—at least, not like this. Whatever the Troll was attempting, it had to be stopped. The air around the creature began to shimmer with dark Mythen, and the ground beneath it cracked as the energy gathered.

"Not on my watch," Therion growled, gripping his sword tightly. With a fierce battle cry, he charged forward. The Troll's glowing eyes fixed on him, its chant growing louder, almost frantic. But Therion was faster. He lunged, driving his blade deep into the Troll's broad chest.

The chant faltered, its sinister rhythm breaking into a gurgling gasp. Dark blood gushed from the wound as the Troll's enormous form slumped to the ground. Its glowing eyes dimmed, the light fading into lifeless orbs. For a moment, there was only silence, the battlefield eerily still around him.

Then the soldiers cheered, their morale surging as they witnessed their commander bring down the beast. They fought with renewed vigor, pushing back the remaining monsters. The tide of battle had turned.

Yet, as Therion stood over the Troll's massive corpse, unease gnawed at him. The creature had been powerful—frighteningly so—and its use of magic was disturbing. But despite its raw strength, it had fallen too easily.

He scanned the battlefield, his gaze lingering on the dying creatures. All of them were going down far too quickly, their resistance weak and uncoordinated. Therion's grip tightened on his sword.

This was supposed to be a threat worthy of Orivera's three strongest companies. But if this was all the enemy had to offer, then something didn't add up. His victory felt hollow, his pride overshadowed by a nagging question—

Was this truly the danger they'd been sent to face— or was the real threat still waiting?

"Commander Wynter!"

Therion turned to see Commander Lysara striding toward him, her silver armor glinting in the firelight. Her long auburn hair was tied back, and her sharp green eyes scanned the battlefield. "You've done it," she said, nodding toward the fallen Troll. "But the monsters aren't retreating."

Therion followed Lysara's gaze. The surviving creatures fought with a frenzied desperation, their shrieks piercing through the chaos of battle. Goblins hurled themselves at his soldiers with wild abandon, and the few remaining direwolves snapped and snarled, refusing to retreat even as arrows pierced their flesh. But their resistance wasn't mere defiance; there was an eerie, purposeful desperation to their fight.

He quickly analyzed the battlefield, his sharp eyes sweeping over the chaos. Most of the monsters clustered at the center of their camp, despite the obvious disadvantage of leaving themselves exposed. It was almost as if they feared losing something vital located there. His mind raced to make sense of it.

"They're defending it," Therion muttered, his tone laced with puzzlement.

"Defending what?" Lysara asked, her voice sharp and urgent as she glanced at him.

Therion's eyes locked onto the center of the clearing, where a grim and grisly sight awaited. Amid the carnage, a mound of bones and blood rose, arranged with unsettling precision. Charred remains were stacked atop shattered skulls, their jagged edges gleaming in the dim light. The macabre display exuded a dark, oppressive energy, making the air feel heavier around them.

"There," Therion said, pointing toward the pile.

Lysara's face hardened as her gaze followed his direction. Without hesitation, she raised her voice above the din of the battlefield. "Mages!" she called, her tone commanding and firm. "Focus fire on that pile! Shield the others!"

The mages sprang into action, forming a tight circle as they chanted in unison. Their Mythen flared to life, glowing with a violent intensity. Moments later, a devastating barrage of fire and lightning streaked through the air, striking the ominous mound. The ground shook violently as the pile erupted in a cloud of smoke and ash, scattering debris across the battlefield.

The monsters howled in agony, their frenzy reaching a fever pitch—then abruptly ceased. A chilling silence fell over the clearing.

Therion shielded his face as thick, acrid smoke billowed outward, accompanied by a putrid stench that turned his stomach. The reek of decay and something far fouler filled the air, nearly forcing him to gag. Before the nausea could overwhelm him, Lysara raised her hands, casting a cleansing spell that swept away the smoke like a gust of wind.

What they saw left the soldiers murmuring in shock.

The bodies of the remaining monsters lay scattered and broken around the smoldering remains. It wasn't the Mythen attack that had felled them directly but their own desperate attempt to shield the mound. Their grotesque corpses formed a grim testament to their determination.

"You were right, Wynter," Lysara said, her voice tinged with disgust. "They were protecting it."

Therion nodded grimly, though unease churned in his gut. "The real question is why."

As he approached the mound, the stench grew stronger, clinging to the air like a living thing. But the smell wasn't what caught his attention. Beneath the charred bones and scorched remains, something unusual gleamed faintly in the firelight. A crude hole had been revealed—its edges clawed and jagged as if dug by monstrous hands. The tunnel descended into the earth, radiating a faint, unnatural glow. A dark pulse of Mythen emanated outward, sending a shiver down Therion's spine.

Commander Vaelrik stormed toward them, his crimson cape billowing behind him. Fury burned in his eyes as he prepared to berate the mages for their wild magical outburst, but he faltered as the stench assaulted his senses. His face twisted with disgust, and his hand instinctively dropped to the hilt of his axe.

"What in the Veil's name is this?" Vaelrik growled as he took in the ominous entrance. "A tunnel?"

Therion knelt at its edge, peering into the oppressive darkness. "The monsters were protecting this," he said, his voice low and measured.

Lysara's frown deepened, her unease evident. "Why? What could be down there?"

Instead of answering, Therion pulled a vial from his satchel. The healing water within shimmered faintly—a blessing from the priests of the Goddess. He poured a small amount onto the tunnel's edge. The liquid hissed and evaporated instantly, leaving behind a trace of black smoke that twisted unnaturally before dissipating.

"Something that shouldn't be," Therion said gravely, his tone heavy with foreboding.

Vaelrik muttered a curse under his breath. "We need to collapse it. Seal whatever's down there."

"No," Therion said firmly as he stood. His gaze never left the tunnel. "If we simply seal it, we might leave a threat to fester beneath us. We need to know what we're dealing with."

Vaelrik's scowl deepened. "You can't be serious, Wynter. Whatever's down there—?"

"Commander Wynter is right," Lysara interrupted, her tone reluctant but resolute. "If we don't investigate, we could be leaving ourselves vulnerable. We need wards and light spells. Mages, prepare for a descent."

Vaelrik's jaw tightened as he glared at her, then at Therion. "This is madness," he growled. "Sealing this pit is the best solution."

"And what if it isn't?" Therion countered, his voice calm but unyielding. "If we don't act now, we may regret it later."

Vaelrik's shoulders sagged as he let out a frustrated sigh. His hand gripped his axe tightly as he pointed a finger at Therion. "Fine. But you'll be leading the way, Wynter."

Therion inclined his head. "Understood."

Lysara gestured for her mages to begin their preparations as Therion unsheathed his blade. The air around them crackled with energy as wards were cast, and faint globes of light hovered near the tunnel's edge.

Garrish, one of the more seasoned warriors, stepped up beside Therion, his expression grim.

"Right beside you, sir," he said, his tone steady despite the tension in the air.

Therion gave him a nod of thanks before turning to Lysara. "Let's move."

***

What had initially appeared to be a crude pit revealed itself to be far more intricate and sinister as they descended deeper into the earth. The rough walls of the upper tunnel soon gave way to a more refined cavern, its surfaces smoothed and carved with an unsettling precision. Strange runes and archaic writings adorned the walls, glowing faintly with a sickly green hue. The symbols pulsed irregularly, casting long, wavering shadows that danced unnervingly in the dim Mythen light conjured by the mages. This was not the work of monsters.

Lysara paused to study the markings, her brow furrowed. "These…" she murmured, running her gloved fingers over the runes. "They're old. Older than anything I've ever seen. But the script is too distorted for me to transcribe. It's almost as if it's deliberately corrupted."

"Corrupted or not," Therion said, his tone sharp, "we need to keep moving. Stay alert."

The oppressive stench of decay intensified as they ventured further, mingled with an unidentifiable rancid odor that made their stomachs churn. The cavern floor was littered with broken bones and the desiccated remains of creatures—evidence of the monsters' presence prior to their arrival. Flies buzzed in the heavy air, their droning an unwelcome accompaniment to the party's cautious footsteps. Garrish grimaced, gripping his weapon tighter. "No monsters left to fight, but it's clear they've been busy. The stench alone could kill a lesser man."

"Quiet," Therion ordered, his voice low. He motioned for the group to halt, raising a hand as he strained to listen. Faintly, over the oppressive silence, he heard it: chanting. Low and guttural, the voices were distorted, as if they were speaking through shredded throats. The sound sent a chill through his spine.

Lysara stepped up to Therion's side, her hand hovering near her staff. "I think I recognize the cadence," she whispered. "The words are slurred and incoherent, but it sounds like an old Mythenian dialect."

"What are they saying?" Therion asked, his voice barely audible.

Lysara's expression tightened. "Come see…" she translated. "Come see the new light."

Her eyes flicked nervously toward the ominous glow ahead.

The party crept forward, their movements slow and deliberate. The chanting grew louder with every step, the voices blending into a discordant, haunting melody that seemed to thrum within their very bones. The glow intensified, revealing a vast chamber ahead. As they stepped into the cavernous space, the sight before them made their blood run cold.

At the center of the chamber stood an altar, its grotesque form carved from black stone that seemed to drink in the faint light around it. Skinned human bodies were sprawled around the altar, their forms contorted in agony. But what turned their faces pale with horror was the realization that these unfortunate souls were not dead. Their chests rose and fell in shallow, labored breaths, and their chanting continued. Their mutilated faces bore no lips, rendering their words garbled and incoherent.

Lysara broke from the group, rushing to one of the damned. She knelt beside the figure, her hands trembling as she tried to assess the extent of their injuries. "They…they're alive," she stammered, her voice shaken. "How is this possible? What could have done this?"

"Lysara, stay back," Therion warned, his hand tightening on his blade. His eyes remained fixed on the glowing altar. There was a palpable energy radiating from it, an unnatural pulse that seemed to worm its way into his mind. A voice whispered at the edge of his consciousness, low and insidious.

Witness… it hissed. *Witness our Lord. He is here.*

Therion groaned, shaking his head to dispel the voice. His vision blurred momentarily, and he stumbled back a step. Garrish, unaware of his commander's turmoil, rushed to Lysara's side, his expression grim.

"Can anything be done for them?" Garrish asked, his voice tight with a mix of hope and dread.

Lysara's hands hovered over the mutilated figure as she cast a minor healing spell, but the magic had no effect. She gasped, recoiling as if burned. "It's no use," she said, her voice trembling. "They've been…tainted. Corrupted by something far beyond our understanding."

The chanting grew louder, their words gaining clarity. Lysara's eyes widened as she finally understood the full phrase. "They're saying, 'Come see the new light. Bear witness. Our Lord is here.'"

"This was a mistake," Therion said, his voice hard and urgent. "We shouldn't be here!"

As if in response to his warning, the chanting abruptly ceased. The mutilated figures began to convulse violently, their bodies writhing on the cold stone floor. Dark, viscous fluid oozed from their wounds, pooling around them in thick rivulets. The fluid moved with a sinister purpose, flowing toward the altar as if drawn by an unseen force.

"Back!" Therion shouted, his voice cutting through the growing chaos. "Everyone, fall back now!"

Lysara stumbled to her feet, retreating as the dark substance climbed the altar, enveloping it in a pulsating black mass. The mages began casting protective wards, their chants frantic as the air grew heavy with malevolent energy.

"Dark Mythen," Lysara whispered, her face pale. "What an ungodly practice…"

"How did monsters learn such a thing?" Vaelrik gasped, his earlier bravado replaced with unease. His axe was raised, but his knuckles were white with tension.

The black pool covering the altar began to shift, the viscous substance slithering and coalescing into an unnatural symbol. The mark glowed with an intense, blinding light that seared itself into their eyes. Then, without warning, the symbol erupted upward in a violent explosion of dark energy.

The shockwave sent them all sprawling, the deafening roar of the blast reverberating through the cavern. Chunks of stone fell from the ceiling, and the ground beneath their feet quaked violently. Therion scrambled to his feet, grabbing Lysara and Garrish by their arms to pull them away as debris rained down around them.

"Move!" he bellowed, his voice hoarse. "We need to get out, now!"

The party fled, the tunnel behind them collapsing as the explosion's shockwaves continued to ripple outward. The oppressive stench of decay and dark magic clung to them as they stumbled back the way they had come, the once-silent walls now filled with the cacophony of destruction.

Therion spared a glance over his shoulder, his heart pounding. The light from the altar had surged upward, a beacon of malice that pierced through the cavern ceiling and into the surface above. He could feel its oppressive presence even as they fled, a tangible weight pressing against his chest.

As the group raced toward the entrance of the cavern, their breaths came ragged, and their boots thundered against the ground. The memory of the grotesque altar and the horrors it unleashed burned fresh in their minds. But as they emerged into the open air, it became chillingly apparent that the nightmare was far from over.

A deafening *boom* shook the earth beneath their feet, a sound so deep it reverberated through their very bones. All heads turned skyward as a massive column of dark energy erupted from the cavern below, shooting high into the heavens. The air itself seemed to ripple with malevolence as the beacon surged ever upward. Therion stood frozen, his knuckles white against the hilt of his blade. The beam of energy pierced the skies, splitting the heavens in a violent explosion of light and shadow. Then, impossibly, it tore through the Veil with a dreadful screech like noise no one had ever heard before.

A thunderous crack followed, and an unnatural silence descended. The men clutched their ears, their faces twisted in pain, as the sky— the very barrier between their world and the unknown— was sundered. Above them hung an unholy rift, a gaping wound that seemed to writhe and pulse like a living thing.

Lysara stumbled forward, her voice trembling as she whispered a prayer. "O'Rivera, shield us in your light," she begged, her hands clutching the emblem of her goddess.

Vaelrik muttered curses under his breath, his usually stoic demeanor shattered by the sight. "The Veil... it's torn... what have we unleashed?"

Their shared horror was interrupted by startled cries from the soldiers.

"Look!" one shouted, pointing to the rift.

From the tear in the Veil, something began to emerge. A shape —impossible and terrible— slithered through the gash, descending with dreadful purpose. It moved with an unnerving form, its form obscured by shadows that seemed to devour the light around it. As it hurtled toward the ground, the soldiers scrambled back, their eyes wide with terror.

"Raise a barrier!" Lysara ordered, her voice sharp despite the tremor in it. The mages acted quickly, pooling their Mythen in a desperate attempt to shield the group. A towering wall of light burst into existence between them and the crash site. The air shimmered with energy as the barrier held firm, though the ground still shook as the unknown object struck with earth-shattering force.

For a moment, all was still. The soldiers gripped their weapons tightly, scanning the smoke-filled crater with bated breath. The Veil above them slowly began to mend itself, the ragged edges knitting together. Relief flickered through the group, but it was short-lived.

From the crash site, a figure began to rise.

The creature stood tall; its form vaguely humanoid but grotesquely distorted. It was faceless, its head smooth and featureless, but its body was an amalgamation of nightmare— blackened skin that seemed to shimmer like molten tar, four elongated arms ending in razor-sharp claws, and a presence so vile it made the air around it feel heavy. It moved forward with an eerie silence, each step deliberate, each movement exuding a malevolence that made their blood run cold.

"What... what is that?" one soldier stammered, his voice barely above a whisper.

No one answered. They could only watch in horrified fascination as the creature approached the barrier. It stopped just before the shimmering wall of light, its head tilting as if studying the humans beyond it. Then, without warning, it raised one of its hands and pressed it against the barrier.

A hiss erupted as the creature's blackened flesh met the light, the skin charring and bubbling upon contact. But it showed no pain, no hesitation. Instead, it pressed harder, its entire body leaning into the barrier. The air around it seemed to warp, and the barrier itself began to waver.

Then, its face— if it could be called that— split open. A grotesque maw lined with rows of jagged, uneven teeth gaped wide, and from within, eyes— unnatural, searing eyes— emerged. They burned like molten gold, locking onto the mages. A wave of psychic pain lashed out, slamming into Lysara and her mages. They cried out in unison, clutching their heads as if their very minds were being torn apart.

"Hold the barrier!" Lysara screamed, her voice breaking. Blood trickled from her nose as she channeled every ounce of her strength into maintaining the wall. "If that thing gets through, we're all doomed!"

Therion's gaze darted between the struggling mages and the creature. "Ready yourselves!" he bellowed to the soldiers. "If it breaks through, we face it head-on!"

Vaelrik turned to him, his face pale with disbelief. "You're mad, Wynter! We should flee otherwise that thing— whatever it is— will slaughter us all!"

"If we turn our backs on it, we die anyway!" Therion shot back. "We have the numbers. We hold the line. Together."

For a moment, Vaelrik was silent, his fear warring with his pride. Finally, he smirked, though the expression was strained. "Some balls you have there, Wynter. Fine. But when we kill this hell spawn, you're buying the wine."

Therion nodded grimly, unsheathing his blade. Garrish stepped forward, his shield raised. "Right beside you, Commander."

The soldiers formed ranks, their weapons ready, and their faces pale but determined. Lysara's mages held on, their chants growing ragged as the creature continued its assault on the barrier. Cracks began to spider web across the shimmering surface, each one accompanied by a pulse of dread.

"It's breaking through!" Lysara shouted, her voice desperate.

"Hold steady!" Therion commanded.

The barrier shattered with a deafening roar, fragments of light scattering like shards of glass. The creature stepped through, its wide maw stitching together to hide its eyes its featureless face. Therion and his knights raised his blades. Knowing this was going to be the hardest battle they'd fought yet.

Chapter Three: An Unforgivable Sin.

All life in the kingdom felt the attack on the Veil…

The Veil was the lifeblood of Orivera, a mystical boundary that separated their realm from the horrors that lurked beyond. It was a constant to the realm, one as vital as the sun and moon. When it tore above the battle at the Shadowed Vale, the sound of its rupture thundered across the kingdom. It was an unholy cacophony, reverberating through the cities and villages as though the people themselves had been dragged to the battlefield to witness its desecration.

Across Orivera, citizens clutched their ears, faces contorted in pain and confusion. Though only for a moment, the air itself felt wrong, vibrating with a chilling resonance that made their stomachs churn and their hearts race. Though they could not comprehend the noise, their bodies reacted instinctively, trembling as if in the presence of a predator they could not see.

In the capital city, Oriana felt it more deeply than anyone else.

To her, the Veil's rupture wasn't just a sound— it was an agonizing blade slicing through her mind. She staggered in her chambers, her polished ceremonial dagger clutched tightly in her hand. The weight of the event pressed against her chest, and her breaths came shallow and quick.

Unlike her people, Oriana knew precisely what had happened. The Veil's tear wasn't a mere accident or anomaly; it was a warning, the prelude to something far worse. Her visions had foretold this moment, though they had been maddeningly vague. She had hoped there would be more time to prepare, to forestall the tragedy she now felt was inevitable.

The doors to her chamber burst open, and three guards stormed in, their faces etched with worry. "Lady Oriana!" one of them called urgently. "Are you unharmed?"

Oriana straightened, hiding the tremor in her hands. "I am fine," she replied, her voice steady despite the storm raging within her. She stepped forward, brushing past the guards. "But the kingdom is not. We have no time to waste. Where are my parents?"

The lead guard hesitated, his brow furrowed. "My lady, the King and Queen are safe. Sir Galen has taken them to the throne room. Please, remain here where it's secure."

"No," Oriana interrupted sharply. "The Castle is not secure— not from what is coming." Her gaze was fierce, her tone leaving no room for argument. "A great tragedy is upon us. If the King and Queen are not fully protected, the kingdom itself will fall. You must do as I say."

The guards exchanged uneasy glances before the leader finally nodded. "Very well. I will rally the remaining troops and secure the castle."

"Good," Oriana said. "Now go."

With that, she turned and marched into the corridor, her two remaining guards trailing close behind her instead. The marble floors echoed with the sharp clatter of their boots, the rhythmic sound only amplifying the urgency in her chest. Oriana's thoughts raced.

Her visions had shown her glimpses of the disaster— the Veil broken, and the forces of the 'Evil Son' sweeping across the land like a plague. Though fragmented, the message was clear enough. The keys— the two halves of the ancient artifact that maintained the Veil's strength— had to be protected. If both halves fell into the wrong hands, Orivera would be lost.

'I thought I had time,' Oriana cursed silently, her jaw clenched. She had already taken precautions. Her half of the key had been entrusted to Rubelle, the one person she trusted above all others. It had been sent far from the castle, out of reach of those who might seek to use it. But the second half— the one her father guarded— remained dangerously close.

And now the Veil had been attacked. The timing was no coincidence.

She knew it was only a matter of time before some foe would come looking for the keys. She pushed herself to move faster, her heart pounding as she neared the throne room. Her parents had to be warned, and the remaining half of the key needed to be secured. A sense of dread gnawed at her. The visions had shown no clear resolution, only the consequences of inaction. For months, she had debated how to approach her parents with what she'd seen. She had not wanted to alarm them without a solution to present. Now, that hesitation felt like a grievous error.

As Oriana approached the grand double doors of the throne room, her heart raced. Each step forward felt heavier, her breath hitching as the muffled voices within grew louder. Her father's commanding tone reached her ears, though the words were indistinct. The doors loomed before her, carved with the sigil of the royal family— a majestic phoenix rising from flames, its wings outstretched as if to protect the realm.

With trembling hands, she pushed the doors open. "Father! Mother!" she cried, her voice filled with urgency.

But her words faltered as she froze in her tracks. The sight before her drained the color from her face and the strength from her knees.

Her father, the mighty King Alaric, knelt in a pool of crimson, his royal robes soaked with his own blood. His eyes, wide with shock and betrayal, were fixed on the lifeless forms of Queen Lysara and Sir Galen, the captain of the royal guard and his closest confidant. The queen's once-vibrant gown clung to her ashen form, and Galen's sword lay discarded beside him, its blade stained.

Standing over them, sword in hand, was Prince Charon. Her Brother.

"Father!" Oriana screamed, her voice cracking. She rushed forward, but one of her guards grabbed her arm, holding her back.

Alaric struggled to raise his head, his trembling hand reaching for the hilt of his sword.

"Charon... why?" he rasped, his voice breaking with the weight of betrayal.

Charon's expression was calm, yet disdain simmered in his eyes. "Why?" he repeated, almost mockingly. "Because you were a weak king, clinging to outdated traditions and blind faith in the Veil. You wouldn't have understood what Ka'rael has promised— a future far greater than this stagnant kingdom."

"You've allied yourself with the 'Fallen Son'?" Alaric spat, his tone laced with pained fury.

Oriana's voice trembled as she stepped forward, her guards flanking her protectively. "You've slaughtered your own blood for the promises of an evil god? How could you?"

Charon's lips curled into a condescending smirk. "You wouldn't understand, dear sister. You've always been so naive. But it doesn't matter.

Once I am king, the realm will flourish in ways you cannot imagine."

"How dare you claim the throne, traitor!" Oriana snapped, her voice fierce despite the tears in her eyes.

"The throne is mine by right," Charon said coldly. "You'd do well to accept that."

Alaric coughed violently, blood staining his lips. "This is a sin... one the Goddess will never forgive." His voice was a whisper, filled with defiance even in his final moments.

Charon's response was swift and merciless. In a single fluid motion, he plunged his blade into Alaric's chest. The king gasped, his body jerking as the life drained from him, before crumpling to the floor.

"No!" Oriana screamed, tears streaming down her face.

Her guards, their rage overpowering their fear, drew their swords and charged at Charon. Determined to do justice in the name of their king, they were too blind to notice how gravely outmatched they were. The Prince did not hesitate, he moved at them with just as much animosity, the clearest difference between them wasn't that he was blue blood and they weren't. It was skill— Skill that made the simplest of his movements look like he had a twisted foresight of their moves before they made them.

As the first guard lunged with his blade aimed at Charon's heart, the Prince countered with a flick of his wrist, parrying the strike, his sword slicing cleanly across the man's throat. The guard dropped to his knees, the strength draining out of him as his blood sprayed across the floor.

The second guard hesitated for moment, a moment that could have spared him his life had he not pressed forward regardless of his fear. A foolish bravery, 'For Orivera!' he must have thought as he raised his sword raised high. Charon sidestepped the blow, twisting the man's arm and pulling him backward into his blade. The guard's expression froze in one of shock, his heart shattering at the realization that he was dying in vain. Thankfully, the pain was only for an instant before his body went limp, sliding off the sword as Charon turned to face Oriana, his expression eerily calm.

Their sacrifices had barely phased the prince, but it'd bought the princess time.

Enough time for Oriana to compose herself and retaliate. She'd staggered back, clutching her ceremonial dagger hidden in her dress. She had always known Charon was a masterful swordsman, but now his movements seemed unnaturally precise, as if guided by some dark force. Her hands steadied with resolve as she began to chant, the ancient words of a spell spilling from her lips.

Mythen swirled around her, its light intensifying with each word.

Charon's eyes narrowed as he realized what she was doing. He raised his sword, preparing to deflect whatever she unleashed, but the spell struck with blinding force, a searing light that sent him crashing into the far wall with a sickening thud.

His body dropped to the floor, his face charred and body smoldering. His chest still heaved, but no man could shrug a blast that strong. Oriana didn't care for his pain. The recoil from the spell she unleashed rocked her body, she panted and swooned, her body trembling from the effort. She wasn't a skilled mage, but she had poured everything into that spell.

Tears rolled down her cheeks as she hid her face. Charon may have betrayed her and the kingdom, but until that moment she'd loved him like any sister should have. She turned to her parents' bodies before the throne. The grief raked through her as she slowly approached them. Crumbling to her knees beside them.

"Please, no," she whispered, her voice choked with sobs. "This wasn't supposed to happen. I could've warned you... I should've warned you."

Her grief was interrupted by a chill that swept through the room. The blood on the marble floor darkened, a sinister miasma rising from it. Oriana's eyes followed the dark tendrils as they coiled toward Charon.

He groaned, his body twitching as the shadows enveloped him, mending his wounds. Slowly, he rose to his feet, his movements jerky and unnatural.

"I didn't think you had it in you to strike me down," Charon said, his voice tinged with something otherworldly.

Oriana's grip tightened on her dagger as she began another chant, but before she could finish, an unseen force struck her hand, sending the weapon clattering to the floor. A sickening snap echoed through the chamber as her fingers bent unnaturally.

"Ahh!" she cried, clutching her hand.

"Don't hurt her!" Charon snapped, his voice directed at no one visible.

Oriana stared at him, tears of pain and confusion streaming down her face. Her brother was arguing with something unseen, his voice filled with anger and desperation.

Oriana's breath caught in her throat as realization dawned. Her lips trembled as she whispered, "Ka'rael…" She looked into her brother's eyes, searching for the boy she once knew. Her voice was barely audible. "Charon… The Fallen Son is lying to you."

Charon shook his head slowly, almost apologetically. His expression softened, but there was an undercurrent of something darker, more resolute. "We have a deal," he said, his tone almost pleading for her understanding. "You wouldn't understand."

Oriana's heart sank. Her knees threatened to give way as tears welled in her eyes. "What deal, Charon?" she demanded, her voice cracking under the weight of her grief. "What could he possibly offer you to make you betray everything? To betray us?"

Charon didn't answer. Instead, he turned towards their father's lifeless form, his steps deliberate, and his face unreadable. The room seemed to hold its breath as he reached down and removed the crown from their father's head. The artifact gleamed even in the dim light, its design intricate yet sinister. The base was forged from blackened iron, its edges lined with jagged filigree that seemed almost alive. Three blood-red jewels were embedded within it, pulsing faintly as though aware of their surroundings. Their light cast eerie patterns on the walls, shifting like liquid fire.

Next, Charon knelt and slipped the ring from their father's stiffened finger. The band was simple in design but bore a similar malevolent energy. The same crimson hue danced within its stone, its glow resonating faintly with the jewels in the crown. Without hesitation, Charon rose and crossed the chamber, his gaze falling on their mother's still form. Oriana could do nothing but watch, paralyzed by despair, as he removed her ring—a delicate band of gold adorned with a matching jewel that gleamed like a shard of captured sunset.

As Charon placed the crown on his head and slid the rings onto his fingers, a surge of energy erupted from the artifacts. The air shimmered, and for a brief moment, the jewels blazed with light, their resonance merging into a single, terrifying harmony. Oriana's chest tightened at the sight, her mind screaming warnings she couldn't voice.

Charon finally turned to face her. His expression was grim, his eyes devoid of the warmth she remembered. "Now," he said, his voice cold and commanding, "where is your half of the key?"

Oriana shook her head, her tears spilling freely. "No… We're not doing that."

"Tell me where it is. Now." He took a step closer, his shadow stretching unnaturally across the floor.

"You think you're still in control," she said, her voice trembling but defiant.

Charon's expression darkened. "Tell me," he demanded, his voice sharper now, "or I will take it by force."

Oriana straightened, summoning the last of her strength. "Go ahead," she growled, her voice low and challenging. "Kill me."

Charon's jaw tightened as his hand shot forward, gripping her neck with an iron grip. He lifted her effortlessly, her feet dangling above the ground. Oriana clawed at his hand, gasping for air as the room seemed to fill with an oppressive weight. The shadows in the chamber deepened, coiling around them like living tendrils.

A cacophony of voices rose around them, low and incomprehensible at first, then gradually forming a sinister chant. *Kill her. Destroy them all.*

Charon winced as the whispers intensified, their words drilling into his mind. His grip faltered for a moment, enough for Oriana to take a shuddering breath. "I'm not… I won't…" he stammered, his voice strained. He closed his eyes tightly, fighting the voices. "Please, sister. I don't want to kill you. You're the only family I have left."

"I won't give you the key," she whispered hoarsely. "We both know what happens when Ka'rael gets what he wants."

Charon's shoulders sagged briefly, a flicker of regret crossing his face. But it vanished as the whispers surged again, louder and more insistent. His expression hardened. "Then you leave me no choice."

The shadows around him grew darker, more tangible. They writhed like serpents, their forms shifting and undulating as though feeding off the despair in the room. A chilling whisper filled the air, low and incomprehensible, like a thousand voices speaking at once. The oppressive force coiled around Oriana, pressing against her chest, tightening like an invisible vice.

Charon lunged forward, his hand gripping her neck once more. This time, the shadows surged alongside him, their tendrils snaking towards her. Oriana's vision blurred as the darkness enveloped her, an inky blackness that seemed to seep into her very being.

The moment the shadows touched her mind, she screamed. It was not a scream of fear but of sheer, unrelenting agony. The invasion was swift and brutal, like a thousand needles piercing her skull. Her thoughts scattered, fragments of memories and emotions tumbling chaotically. The shadows probed deeper, rummaging through her mind with cruel efficiency.

Oriana fought back, trying to bury her thoughts, to shield the secrets they sought. But the more she resisted, the worse the pain became. It was as though the needles twisted and burrowed further, digging into the deepest recesses of her consciousness. The sensation was suffocating, an unbearable pressure that left her gasping for air.

She could feel the darkness, cold and alien, sifting through her memories. Each touch was invasive, leaving a trail of burning pain in its wake. Her childhood flashed before her eyes, followed by moments of joy, sorrow, and love—each one torn apart by the relentless shadows. She tried to focus, to push them away, but the effort only drained her further.

"Stop," she gasped, tears streaming down her face. Her voice was weak, barely more than a whisper. "Please…"

Charon's eyes flickered with something— hesitation, perhaps— but it was quickly overshadowed by the cold resolve that had consumed him. The whispers grew louder, a deafening chorus that drowned out all other sound.

Make her speak her truth.

Charon murmured something in an ancient tongue, the words foreign and guttural. The shadows responded, their movements becoming more frenzied. Oriana cried out as the invasion reached its peak, the pain blinding and all-consuming. She felt her strength fading, her will crumbling under the relentless assault.

But even as the darkness threatened to overwhelm her, a spark of defiance remained. She clung to it desperately, shielding what little she could from the probing shadows. Her breathing was ragged, her body trembling, but she refused to give in.

Charon's grip tightened, his face a mask of frustration. "Where is it?" he demanded, his voice cutting through the whispers. "Tell me, Oriana. I don't want to hurt you any more than I already have."

Oriana met his gaze, her eyes blazing with defiance even as her strength waned.

"I-it's not— no… not here…" She rasped, biting her own lip. "No... I won't..."

She choked, blood trickling from her nose as she resisted.

"You're hurting yourself." Charon barked, his voice amplified by the sinister force surrounding him. "Tell me where, and I'll make **it** stop."

The more Oriana resisted, the more unbearable the agony became. Her body convulsed as if her very essence were being wrung dry. Every muscle trembled, her breath came in ragged gasps, and her mind spiraled into chaos. She fought against the darkness invading her thoughts, but the harder she pushed back, the sharper the pain became— like needles driven slowly into her brain, accompanied by an oppressive weight crushing her chest.

It felt foreign, invasive, and cruel, rummaging through her mind like a thief sifting through precious treasures. She tried to bury her thoughts deeper, concealing them beneath layers of memories and emotions, but the effort only intensified the torment.

Oriana didn't even realize when the words began to spill from her lips, unbidden.
"It's… not with me," she gasped through the pain, tears streaming down her face. Her voice cracked, barely above a whisper. "I sent it away… to… I can't! I won't tell you where."

Her resolve wavered as she bit her tongue hard, drawing blood to silence herself, but it was too late. The instant the thought crossed her mind, the shadows seized it greedily.

"Rubelle."

The name echoed in a symphony of cruel whispers, taunting and jeering, reverberating in the oppressive chamber like a twisted hymn. Charon furrowed his brows at the sound, his expression hardening as the truth clicked into place.

"You sent the key away with the Court Mage," he said, his tone a mix of revelation and frustration. "Where?"

Oriana could barely hear him over the roaring in her ears. The pain had stolen her voice, leaving her gasping and trembling on the floor. She tried to speak, but her body had reached its limit.

Charon's eyes widened as he realized the toll his actions had taken. With an angry growl, he shoved her away, breaking the darkness's hold on her. Oriana crumpled to the cold marble floor, clutching at her chest as she gulped in air.

He frowned as he stared down at her. Once, he had admired his sister's unyielding will, her fierce determination to protect their people. But now, her defiance felt like nothing more than a barrier to his purpose— a stubborn refusal to see the greater picture.

The whispers snapped at him, their hissing voices demanding more. Charon clenched his fists, his frustration mounting. "We know who has it," he muttered, his voice defiant. "I'll find her on my own."

The chamber doors burst open with a thunderous crash, and a flood of knights poured into the room. They froze in their tracks, their expressions a mixture of confusion and horror at the sight before them. The lifeless forms of the King and Queen lay sprawled at the base of their thrones, their regalia stripped from their bodies. The Knight Commander, their trusted leader, lay slain beside them.

Charon turned to face the intruders, his imposing figure framed by the eerie glow of the resonating jewels he now wore.

"My father is dead," he declared, his voice carrying a chilling finality. "I am your ruler now. Kneel before me."

The knights exchanged uncertain glances, their initial shock giving way to fury. They had pledged their lives to the crown, but they would not bow to a traitor. The bravest among them stepped forward, swords drawn, ready to avenge their fallen monarchs.

Charon raised his hand, his expression cold and unyielding. The jewels on the crown and rings pulsed with energy, their glow intensifying as he invoked their power. A word, heavy with the weight of a royal Mythen, thundered through the chamber.

"Kneel!"

The command struck like a physical blow, compelling every knight to the ground. Their weapons clattered to the floor as an invisible force crushed their resistance. None of them had ever experienced such authority before; most had not even known the royal bloodline possessed this power. They struggled against it, but their bodies refused to obey their will, submitting to the overwhelming compulsion.

Oriana, struggling to remain conscious, lifted her head weakly. Her vision blurred, her gaze fixed on her brother as despair filled her heart.

"Dear O'Rivera," she whispered, her voice barely audible. "Help us…"

Her thoughts turned to Rubelle, her last shred of hope. But as her strength gave out, her head fell against the marble floor, and darkness claimed her.

***

It was hard to believe that only moments ago, the castle had been alive with a cacophony of sound— the bustle of staff, and the march of heavy armored guards patrolling the halls. Now, an eerie silence hung over the halls like a shroud. Behind closed doors, the servants mourned their lost monarchs in hushed tones, seeking solace in shadows where they believed they were safe from their new King's wrath.

Not that Charon would have blamed them.

His parents were not cruel rulers. They had been just and beloved by many, and he harbored no hatred for them. If anything, he loved them deeply. But love did not outweigh the demands of the realm. He would not punish their loyal subjects for their grief, as long as none of them entertained dangerous notions of vengeance or justice. The mere thought of rebellion, however small, could not be allowed to fester.

Even so, a pang of sorrow struck his chest. He already missed his mother's serene wisdom and his father's steady guidance. But Charon reminded himself, they would have never allowed him to do what was necessary. What he had done. The burden of his actions settled like iron on his shoulders, and for the first time, doubt crept in like a cold whisper. Could there have been another way?

His frown deepened as he shifted Oriana in his arms, cradling her fragile form. The dimly lit corridors stretched endlessly before him, each flickering torch casting jagged shadows on the walls. His sister's head rested against his shoulder, her breaths shallow but steady. Her ordeal had taken a visible toll, her pallor ashen, her body unnaturally still. Yet she lived. That was all that mattered.

Charon pushed the thought of regret from his mind. He'd come too far. Success was within reach, and there could be no turning back now.

"Summon your new Knights Commander," he ordered as they approached the grand double doors of Oriana's chambers. The guards at their post straightened, their faces masked with stoic professionalism. "No one is to enter until he arrives."

The knights bowed and stepped aside to open the doors for him, their movements precise. The heavy oak groaned as it swung inward, revealing the opulence of the princess's private quarters— silken drapes, a gilded vanity, and the faint lingering scent of lavender.

Charon entered without hesitation, the door shutting firmly behind him. The room, for all its luxury, felt cold, lifeless, much like the rest of the castle. He crossed the room in long strides and carefully laid Oriana down upon her bed. The silken sheets whispered as he pulled them over her small frame, ensuring she was shielded from the night's chill.

It was a gesture he'd performed countless times over the years, a habit born of care for his younger sister. Yet, in this moment, it felt hollow. She would not see the kindness in it. When she awoke, she would see only the betrayal.

Charon stepped back, his gaze lingering on her pale face. Despite everything, there was still an innocence to her, a fragility he wanted desperately to protect— even from himself.

He paused, watching her for a moment. Her chest rose and fell in an unsteady rhythm, her face serene despite the tumult she had endured. She looked so much like their mother when she was at peace. It was a small comfort, one that he didn't deserve.

Charon's gaze shifted to the bedside table, where he contemplated leaving her ceremonial dagger that he'd picked up after the incident at the throne room. The blade, gifted to Oriana by

Rubelle when her mythen training began, shimmered faintly in the room's dull lighting. He reached out, his fingers brushing the hilt, and hesitated.

It was a beautiful weapon, expertly crafted and engraved with protective runes. But now, as his hand lingered over it, he recalled the spell she'd almost killed him with and wondered if it was too dangerous to leave in her possession. The thought unsettled him. He caught his reflection in the polished surface of a nearby mirror and grimaced.

The face staring back at him was weary, hardened, and unfamiliar. His features, once noble and proud, now bore the weight of a man who feared his dearest sister would one day try to kill him.

Charon turned away, unable to face his own reflection. Instead, he focused on Oriana. Her hair was splayed across the pillow like a silken halo, and he reached out, brushing a stray strand from her face. His calloused fingers moved with a gentleness that felt foreign, almost alien, amidst the weight of the day's horrors.

He lingered for a moment, allowing himself this fleeting softness. But the world did not permit such indulgences for long.

Kill her… kill her…

The voice hissed and plead announcing the new unwelcome presence in the room. The air in the room shifted, thickening with an unnatural weight. The light from the hearth dimmed as the shadows lengthened, coiling like serpents in the corners of the chamber. They stretched and twisted, their edges flickering with a life of their own.

Charon's jaw tightened, his teeth grinding audibly.

"You can hiss and whisper all you like," he growled lowly, his voice filled with menace, "but I will not harm her."

The multitude of voices that usually accompanied the darkness fell silent. Then, one deep, resonant voice emerged, cold and mocking.

"Not harm her? You killed your own parents, Charon. What makes her so different?"

Charon's fists tightened, his nails digging into his palms. He squared his shoulders, his glare fixed on the shadow.

"They were too attached to the old ways," he snapped. "They were blind, unwilling to see what needs to be done for Orivera to survive. Oriana… she's different. She will understand."

He turned back to his sister, stroking her hair absently, his voice softening. "She's always understood."

The shadow laughed, a taunting sound that sent a shiver down Charon's spine and made his blood boil.

"Different?" it sneered. "She resisted you, defied you, and still withholds what you seek. She's no different from them."

Charon's lip curled in a snarl. "You were in her head. You must know where Rubelle is going."

The shadow shifted, its edges rippling like water disturbed by an unseen force. Its voice dropped to a conspiratorial murmur. "She held firm. Even I could not pry it from her."

Charon's scowl deepened, but the shadow's next words froze him.

"Maybe you could help me… to help you."

He stiffened, the insinuation clear. His mind raced, but before he could respond, the chamber door creaked open. He turned sharply to see a young knight entering, his armor polished but slightly ill-fitted, betraying his nervous energy. His dark hair was cropped close, and his hazel eyes burned with suppressed anger and unease.

The young man dropped to one knee, bowing stiffly. "Your Majesty," he said, his voice steady despite the tension in his frame. "You summoned me."

Charon recognized him, his father was a hero who'd served alongside Sir Galen. He imagined the boy must have despised him for what he'd done. 'Good' he thought to himself as he studied him for a moment. He had no need for a knight that was either too eager to serve or too afraid of his power either. "Sir Aedric, as the next Knight Commander, you will serve as my personal guard and see to it that my orders are met quickly and efficiently. Do you understand this?"

"Yes… Your Majesty." He replied coldly.

"Assemble a search party immediately. Send word to ensure the Walls are secured and ensure no one leaves the Capital. The Court Mage, Rubelle, has stolen something of great importance to my family. I will not rest until it is returned." King Charon demanded.

Aedric's brows furrowed briefly, but he nodded sharply. "It will be done, Your Majesty."

"Good." Charon's tone was curt. "Now go."

Aedric rose, bowing once more before excusing himself. As the door clicked shut behind him, Charon exhaled slowly, turning his gaze to the balcony. He walked toward it, the cool noon air brushing against his skin as he stepped out. The city sprawled before him, so bright and wonderfully oblivious to the darkness that has festered within the palace walls.

He raised his hand, the jewels on his crown and rings glowing faintly in response. The shadows around him seemed to vibrate with anticipation, their presence growing stronger. The deep voice returned, its tone mocking yet insistent.

"Let's see what you can manage with half the key," it said, the words slithering into his ears.

Charon ignored it, focusing on the veil that separated their world from the unknown beyond. He could feel it, a barrier both delicate and unyielding, pulsating with energy. He reached out with his will, the jewels amplifying his power.

The veil quivered, and for a moment, it felt as though he could pierce through it. Slowly, a rift began to form, a jagged tear in the fabric of reality. A dark, shapeless mass slipped through, its form indistinct but radiating malevolence.

Suddenly, the veil retaliated, its energy surging back with a force that sent Charon flying backward as it thundered. A noise more violent that the sound it made when it'd first ripped. It was a sound and a feeling all at once, as the first had forced the people to cover their ears, this time it made every cell in their bodies scream though only for a second. Charon roared in pain as he fell to the ground inside Oriana's room. She may have been unconscious but the pain etched her features as he writhed on the ground for a moment. The pain was instant for everyone else, but for him it felt as though the jewels on his body amplified it, punishing for attempting to control the veil while he did not hold the complete key. He wailed as he shook the crown of his head and pried the rings off his fingers.

All while the shadows laughed.

"I need the full key," he let out, furious and winded y the recoil. " Otherwise I won't do that again!"

The shadow loomed over him, its edges curling in amusement. "No worries… You've done enough for now," it assured him, its tone dripping with satisfaction. Charon glared at the darkness, but before he could retort, the oppressive presence vanished, leaving him alone on the balcony.

Chapter Four: The Escape

*Unaware that the Prince had declared her a fugitive,
Rubelle rode out of the main city toward the Wall on its
outskirts…*

Dalia was asleep now, thankfully so. When the first wave of energy from the veil's rip washed over them it'd sent the girl and horse into a panic. She herself was rattled, but managed to keep everything under control. Though it'd set them back several minutes as she couldn't continue their journey until she'd calmed her daughter enough. Now they were back on track and she couldn't stop thinking about what had happened. She'd told herself it was a singular anomaly, something distant and done.

She was still trying to make sense of what they'd felt before they were hit by the second more violent wave.

In an instant the air around them turned heavy, pregnant with an unnatural stillness that made the hairs on Rubelle's neck rise. Then it came— a gut-wrenching, ear-splitting crackling noise like thunder that ripped through the sky like the earth itself protesting its existence. The sound reverberated through the air, more oppressive than the first wave, and sent a ripple of unease coursing through every fiber of Rubelle's being. The force hit her chest like a blow, knocking the breath from her lungs.

Her horse reared violently, a terrified scream tearing from its throat as its front hooves lashed at the air. Rubelle's instincts took over as she gripped the reins tightly with one hand and clutched Dalia with the other. Her daughter whimpered, burying her face into Rubelle's tunic, her small body trembling.

"Easy! Easy, boy!" Rubelle cried, her voice straining as she leaned forward to calm the animal.

The reins burned against her palms, but she held firm, whispering frantic words of comfort. "It's alright… It's alright…"

The horse's panic was contagious. Rubelle could feel her own heart thundering in her chest as she fought to steady the beast. Her legs pressed tightly into the saddle, her focus entirely on keeping them upright. The horse bucked again, its fear almost unbearable, but Rubelle refused to let go.

"Mama!" Dalia's shriek broke through the cacophony. She was awake again, and terrified too. "What's happening?!"

"It's okay!" Rubelle gasped, though her voice cracked under the strain. "Hold on tight, my love! Just hold on!"

After what felt like an eternity, the horse began to calm, its hooves stamping nervously against the ground. Rubelle's trembling fingers stroked its mane, her murmured reassurances growing softer as the animal's breathing slowed. She could feel its terror mirrored in her own quaking limbs, but the immediate danger had passed.

Rubelle slumped forward in the saddle, her forehead resting against the horse's neck as the tension drained from her body. Her arms ached from holding Dalia secure, but she refused to let go.

"Mama…" Dalia's voice was a broken whisper. She pulled back just enough for Rubelle to see the tears streaking her dirt-smudged cheeks. "It happened again… like before…"

Rubelle's heart sank. The girl had tried to be brave after the first wave, even holding her composure despite the unnatural disturbance. But this second one— the sheer violence of it— had unraveled that fragile courage.

"I know," Rubelle murmured, brushing a lock of hair from her daughter's tear-streaked face. Her voice was low and unsteady, her smile thin and forced. "I felt it too. But it's over now. We're safe."

The words tasted bitter in her mouth. She had felt it just as keenly as Dalia, the terrible wrongness of the energy that had torn through the sky. This was no accident, no mere coincidence. Something— or someone— was meddling with forces beyond their comprehension.

The first wave had been a warning, a tremor signaling that the Veil had been tampered with. But this? This was intentional. This second rupture felt precise, calculated as if someone, or something, had deliberately clawed at the fabric separating their world from the horrors beyond. Rubelle tightened her hold on Dalia, her jaw set in determination. She couldn't let fear consume her; there was too much at stake.

Her gaze lifted to the horizon, back toward the royal city and the castle that loomed at its center. The spires rose like solemn sentinels against the darkening sky, their once reassuring presence now a reminder of what could be lost. Her chest tightened painfully as her thoughts turned to Princess Oriana. Rubelle's mission had been of utmost importance even before this strange event, but now her urgency felt like a physical weight pressing down on her chest.

"The princess will be alright," she told herself firmly, though doubt gnawed at the edges of her resolve. She imagined Oriana's kind eyes and determined smile, the way she carried herself with both grace and strength. The thought of harm befalling her was unbearable. Yet Rubelle knew she couldn't afford to dwell on it. Her focus had to remain on the task at hand.

"Do you think the princess heard it too?" Dalia asked softly, her voice trembling as she followed her mother's gaze toward the distant spires of the castle. "Do you think they're okay?"

Rubelle hesitated, her grip tightening slightly on the reins. She understood her daughter's concern; Dalia had accompanied her to the castle a few times, and the princess had always been so kind to her, going out of her way to make the girl feel welcome. That kindness had left a deep impression on Dalia, and Rubelle wasn't surprised that her thoughts turned to the princess now, even amidst her own fear.

"The castle is protected by powerful wards," Rubelle said, her voice steady despite the unease gnawing at her. "And the best soldiers in the kingdom guard its walls. It's the safest place there is."

"I'm sure not just Oriana, but the King and Queen are all safe."

Dalia's brows furrowed. "Then why are we leaving?"

Rubelle forced a smile, though it felt fragile on her lips. "Because we've got a job to do, darling. Important work." Even as she spoke, doubt crept into her thoughts. She knew they had to leave, but the specifics of their mission were still shrouded in uncertainty. She trusted her instincts, though, and the urgency of the Veil's disturbance left no room for hesitation.

"I'm worried about Daddy," Dalia pouted, her voice small but laced with heartbreak.

Rubelle's heart clenched. She'd thought of Therion too, of the panic he'd feel when he returned to find them gone. He'd be worried—angry, even. But things couldn't have gone any other way. "We'll see him soon," she promised, though the words felt heavy. "I promise, love. Everything will be alright."

Dalia nodded, though her expression remained troubled. She buried her face in Rubelle's chest, seeking comfort in her mother's embrace. Rubelle stroked her hair gently, whispering reassurances that she hoped were true.

But even as she comforted her daughter, unease clung to Rubelle like a shadow. Her mind raced with thoughts of the old stories; the warnings passed down about the Veil that separated their world from the Fallen Son's domain. The Veil being tampered with had been deemed impossible by scholars and sages alike. And yet, the sound and force of the rip were undeniable— a haunting confirmation that the impossible had become real.

Reaching into her cloak, Rubelle felt for the precious gem entrusted to her care. Its smooth, cool surface against her fingertips brought a sliver of reassurance. The gem was their only hope, though its full purpose was still a mystery to her. All she knew was that she had to protect it, no matter the cost. Urging the horse forward once more, she glanced over her shoulder, scanning the road behind them. It was empty, the fields stretching in peaceful silence. Yet she couldn't shake the feeling that they were being watched.

"Mama, are we almost there?" Dalia's voice broke through her thoughts, muffled against Rubelle's chest.

"Yes, my love," Rubelle replied softly. Her words were more prayer than promise. In her heart, she whispered a plea to O'Rivera, the Goddess of Light, for guidance and protection. Surely, the divine would not abandon them now.

The road began to incline, and Rubelle urged the horse to quicken its pace. She could see the faint outline of the city walls in the distance, still several miles away but a glimmer of hope nonetheless. Her thoughts turned back to the sound of the rip—a horrifying noise that lingered at the edge of her mind. It was an experience no living being in the realm could forget so easily.

"Just a little further," Rubelle murmured, more to herself than to the horse. The gathering darkness seemed to press against her, and her gaze darted to the shadows along the roadside. Every rustle of leaves felt like a threat, every whisper of wind a warning. She gripped the reins tighter, her resolve hardening.

Whatever had caused the Veil's disturbance, she had to believe the capital would stand strong against it. But even as she clung to that hope, she knew this was only the beginning. The Veil was in danger, and something far worse was bound to follow. Rubelle squared her shoulders and pressed on, reminding herself that above all she had her daughter's safety to worry about.

***

Lysara stood at the edge of the formation, her once-pristine robes now bloodied and torn, though her resolve remained unbroken. Her voice rang out over the din of battle, sharp and clear like a clarion call. "On my mark, release the barrier!" she commanded, her eyes briefly darting toward the knights gathered behind her. "Commander Therion, you lead the charge!"

Therion nodded, his expression hard and resolute. His silver armor was streaked with grime and blood, evidence of the fierce struggle that had already taken place. Around him, the knights of Orivera shifted their stances, shields interlocking as they formed a phalanx around the mages. Despite the odds, their determination was unwavering.

Behind the shield wall, Lysara and her fellow mages concentrated, their hands glowing with arcane energy as they channeled power into the shimmering barrier that protected the formation. Sweat beaded on Lysara's brow, but she held firm, her hands weaving intricate patterns that maintained the shield against the relentless onslaught.

"Now!" she shouted, her voice cutting through the chaos like a whip crack. With a final twist of her hands, the barrier began to dissipate, its radiant energy unraveling into the ether.

The Hellspawn reacted instantly. The creature lunged forward, its massive form moving with a speed that defied its bulk. Claws like scythes sliced through the air, seeking flesh to rend and tear. Therion roared, stepping forward with his great sword raised high. The blade gleamed as it arced downward, striking the creature's side.

Behind him, the knights surged, their cries a symphony of defiance. They thrust their spears toward the beast, their precision remarkable despite the chaos. Yet their weapons seemed pitifully ineffective; the creature's hide was unnaturally resilient, and though a few spears pierced its flesh, the wounds closed almost immediately, knitting themselves together as though the Hellspawn were mocking their efforts.

Therion gritted his teeth and pressed forward, slashing again and again. His sword bit into the creature's side, carving deep gashes—but to his dismay, the wounds healed faster than he could inflict them. He leaped back as the creature retaliated, its claws raking the air where he had stood moments before.

"Pincer the abomination!" Therion bellowed, his voice carrying above the clash of steel. His strategy was clear: if they couldn't kill it outright, they would overwhelm it, exploiting every angle and driving their spears relentlessly into its flesh.

The knights obeyed, surrounding the Hellspawn with practiced precision. Their spears jabbed and pierced, keeping the creature occupied and forcing it to divide its attention. Therion glanced back toward Lysara, their eyes meeting across the battlefield.

"How much longer?" he shouted, desperation creeping into his tone.

Lysara didn't break her focus, her hands glowing with a brilliant blue light as she and the other mages prepared their spell. "We need more time! Hold the line!"

Her words were drowned out by a bloodcurdling scream. Therion turned, his heart sinking as he saw shields splintering and knights being flung into the air like ragdolls.

The Hellspawn had adapted. With terrifying speed, it began snatching spears and shields from its attackers, wielding the stolen weapons with unsettling precision. It moved like a whirlwind, striking with the brutal efficiency of a seasoned warrior. In one clawed hand, it held a long sword; in another, a shield. A third claw gripped a spear, and the fourth remained free, slashing with feral ferocity.

"Damn it all!" barked Commander Vaelrick, a grizzled veteran clad in ornate black armor. He signaled to one of his Dracoseekers, elite knights trained to subdue the kingdom's most dangerous foes. As the Hellspawn lunged, Vaelrick charged, his blade gleaming in the dim light.

The beast swung its spear toward him in a deadly arc, but a Dracoseeker intercepted, parrying the blow with a well-timed strike. Vaelrick ducked low, narrowly avoiding a swipe from the creature's claw, and rose with a powerful slash. His blade severed one of its legs, sending the Hellspawn crashing to the ground.

The knights pulled back, regrouping around their commanders but with their eyes still trained on the monster. Vaelrick stood panting, his sword raised defensively as he watched the creature writhe on the ground.

"Is it dead?" one knight asked hesitantly, his voice tinged with hope.

"No," Therion growled, his eyes fixed on the Hellspawn. Even as they watched, the severed limb began to regenerate, sinew and muscle knitting themselves together with horrifying speed. The creature lay still for a moment, its featureless face staring blankly at them as if taunting their efforts.

Vaelrick spat on the ground. "It's like fighting a Colossus," he muttered, frustration etched into his features. "But at least those scaly bastards bleed."

Therion glanced at Lysara, his brow furrowed. "If we can't kill it, how do we stop it?"

Vaelrick smirked, a glimmer of confidence returning to his eyes.

"We capture it," he declared. "I've already signaled for the Dragon Net. Its enchanted silver is strong enough to hold fully mature wyvern— it should be strong enough to hold this abomination long enough for us to figure out how to destroy it."

"What makes you so sure that would work?" Therion retorted.

"Do you have a better idea?" Vaelrick hissed.

Lysara nodded, her hands still moving in intricate patterns as she and the other mages chanted. The energy around them intensified, the air crackling with power. "We'll support you," she said firmly interrupting them. "It's risky but Vaelrick and his Dracoseekers are the most experienced in combating monsters of this caliber."

Therion reluctantly agreed as she turned to face the weathered commander. "We'll strike on your command."

Vaelrick turned to his allies. "When that thing charges, we'll hit it with everything we've got. Once it's down, the net goes over it, and we finish this. For O'Rivera! For Honor!"

The knights braced themselves, their weapons at the ready as they chanted his war cry.

For O'Rivera! For Honor!

Despite their fatigue, hope flickered in their eyes. The Plan was simple and everyone understood their roles.

Unfortunately, their plan was in vain.

Sure enough the Hellspawn rose with an unsettling grace, its grotesque form twisting as it regained its footing.— but it did not charge at them. Instead its featureless face split apart again, reminding them of the unholy visage behind its blank expression. Therion was the only one that noticed the odd glint in its eyes, they seemed to pulse with malevolent intelligence. It wasn't just a beast driven by primal rage; it was calculating. **Aware**.

The realization hit Therion like a blow to the chest.

"It knows," he murmured, barely above a whisper, and following its gaze he found it was fixated on the Mages chanting their next attack. His instincts screamed, and he lunged toward Lysara, tackling her to the blood-soaked ground. "Find cover!" His shout rang out, sharp and desperate.

No sooner had the words left his mouth than the air froze with a palpable chill. A wave of destructive mythen erupted from the Hellspawn, tearing through the ranks of the knights before it and devastating the Arcane Vanguard they'd tried to shield. The blast was not a crude burst of power; it was focused, deliberate, and devastating. The protective shields of the mages shattered like brittle glass, and their screams were swallowed in an inferno of dark energy.

When the chaos subsided, the once-ordered battlefield was a graveyard. Charred bodies lay strewn across the ground, their blood soaking into the earth. Lysara blinked, her ears ringing, her body trembling as she pushed herself upright. Only a few mages remained standing— those who had heeded Therion's warning in time.

Vaelrick staggered to his feet, his expression one of shock and fury. His usually sharp commands faltered, replaced by a grim mutter. "This... this is no beast. It's a demon from the Abyss itself."

The Hellspawn stood amidst the carnage, surveying its handiwork. Its many eyes narrowed, its gaze fixed on the survivors with a chilling sense of satisfaction. Then, it began to fire again, each beam of dark mythen ripping through the lines, leaving little time to mourn or regroup.

Lysara, trembling with grief and rage, stood despite her injuries. The weight of her losses pressed against her chest like an iron vice. Over a hundred mages had marched into this battle, yet now only a handful remained. Tears streamed down her face as she screamed drawing the Hellspawn's attention to herself, "Enough!"

Her voice carried the weight of despair and unrelenting fury.

She thrust her hands forward, conjuring a massive surge of her own mythen. The golden energy crackled and flared, colliding with the Hellspawn's next attack. The impact sent shockwaves rippling across the field, forcing both combatants to stagger.

The creature faltered for the first time, its many eyes widening as Lysara hurled another bolt of energy. It retaliated with inhuman speed, kicking a discarded spear toward her with devastating force. She barely managed to conjure a shield, but the impact drove the weapon into her side, piercing her flesh. A strangled gasp escaped her lips as she fell to one knee.

Her attack, however, found its mark. The mythen struck the Hellspawn's shoulder, searing through its grotesque flesh in a wound so severe it'd crippled the hand at the joint. The wound hissed and crackled, refusing to heal. The beast shrieked in agony, the sound a discordant symphony of rage and pain.

Therion rushed to Lysara's side, panic etched on his bloodied face. "You're injured! You need—"

"Magic hurts it!" Lysara rasped, cutting him off. Her voice was hoarse but resolute. "Enchant your blades! Strike it down while you can!"

Her words reignited a flicker of hope in the battered survivors. Therion stood, his chest heaving, and bellowed to the remnants of his forces, "Knights of Orivera! To arms! Enchant your weapons and shields!"

The remaining mages, battered and weary, poured the last of their strength into enchanting the knights' gear. The battlefield shimmered with renewed energy as swords, spears, and shields glowed with a faint, divine light.

The Hellspawn, sensing the shift in the tide, unleashed another wave of dark energy. But this time, the enchanted shields absorbed the brunt of the attack. The knights surged forward, their resolve hardened by desperation. They surrounded the creature, striking with weapons imbued with the searing power of mythen.

The beast retaliated with unrelenting ferocity. Its claws tore through armor, its movements a deadly blur. Yet the enchanted blades bit deep, leaving wounds that refused to heal. A battle of attrition unfolded, each side testing the limits of their endurance.

Vaelrick, ever the strategist, seized the moment. He darted forward, his sword glowing like molten silver. With a swift, calculated strike, he severed one of the Hellspawn's arms. The creature howled, staggering under the assault. But before he could retreat to safety, it lashed out with its remaining claws, snatching him by the torso.

"Vaelrick!" Therion's voice cracked with desperation as he watched the commander struggle in the creature's grip. The Hellspawn's maw opened wide, and with a sickening crunch, it silenced

Vaelrick's final battle cry. His lifeless body was discarded like a broken doll, his blood staining the earth.

The knights faltered, their morale wavering at the loss of their leader. The Hellspawn turned its attention to the remaining warriors, its wounds slowly mending. It began to retreat, clearly intent on escaping and recovering fully before returning to finish them off.

Therion would not allow it.

He snatched a nearby spear, its tip still glowing with enchantment, and hurled it with all his might. The weapon struck true, piercing the Hellspawn's back. The creature roared, its movements faltering as Therion charged.

He tackled the beast, driving it to the ground. The two grappled in a brutal struggle, each blow from the Hellspawn a thunderous impact against his battered armor. Blood streamed from a gash on his head where a claw had torn away his helmet, but he pressed on. His sword slashed across its torso, carving deep, glowing wounds into its dark flesh.

The Hellspawn, now unarmed and desperate, lunged with renewed ferocity. It knocked Therion to the ground, pinning him beneath its monstrous weight. Its claws hovered inches from his throat, ready to end him.

With a roar of defiance, Therion summoned the last reserves of his strength. He drove his blade upward, plunging it into the creature's chest. The enchanted steel burned as it pierced through the Hellspawn's core.

The creature let out a final, earsplitting shriek. Its body convulsed violently, then began to disintegrate. Dark tendrils of energy spiraled away, dissipating into the air like smoke from a dying fire.

By the time its form crumbled to ash, only silence remained.

Therion collapsed beside the smoldering remnants, his chest heaving with exhaustion. Blood dripped from his wounds, pooling beneath him. Around him, the battlefield was eerily quiet, save for the labored breathing of the few survivors.

Lysara approached, clutching her side where the spear had struck. Her face was pale, her steps unsteady, but her gaze was resolute. She knelt beside Therion, placing a trembling hand on his shoulder.

"We did it," she murmured, her voice heavy with both relief and sorrow.

Therion forced a weak smile, though his eyes betrayed the weight of their losses. "At what cost?" he whispered.

They surveyed the carnage around them. The once-proud knights of Orivera were reduced to a handful of battered warriors. The Arcane Vanguard and Dracoseekers, once a pair of the most formidable forces in all of Orivera, were nearly annihilated. Vaelrick's body lay among the fallen too, a grim reminder of the price they had paid. They'd survived, but this was no victory.

***

As Rubelle and Dalia finally made it to the City's Walls…

It stretched impossibly high, its surface glinting with enchanted runes that shimmered faintly even in daylight, a perpetual warning to any who dared challenge its defenses. The gates, wrought of polished steel reinforced with veins of gold, bore intricate carvings depicting the kingdom's victories and legends. Gargoyle-like statues lined the battlements, like scarecrows for most monsters that'd wandered too close from time to time.

Rubelle rode toward the gates with determination, her daughter nestled against her chest, her small arms gripping tightly. The Sun had set, yet even out of sight it still cast the wall in a warm glow that made it appear almost ethereal. Rubelle had no time to admire its beauty. She reached the gate and pulled her horse to a halt as the knights stationed there stepped forward.

"Halt! State your business," barked one of the knights, his polished armor gleaming.

Rubelle lifted her chin, producing a small, intricately engraved phoenix emblem from a pouch at her side. The golden bird was the symbol of the Elyndrals, their ruling monarchs.

"I am Rubelle Wynter, the court mage, on urgent business by the order of Princess Oriana," she declared, her voice steady but firm.

The knights exchanged uneasy glances. "Court mage or not, protocol dictates that you provide clearance for entry."

Rubelle's eyes narrowed, her patience thinning. "That emblem is my clearance. Unless you wish to delay matters of state importance, I suggest you step aside."

The lead knight hesitated but eventually motioned for the gates to be opened. With a groan, the enormous steel doors parted, revealing a small passage leading to the inner gate. Rubelle nudged her horse forward, her daughter clutching her cloak tightly as they passed through the first threshold.

As soon as they were inside, the inner gate slammed shut behind them with a resounding clang. Rubelle stopped her horse abruptly, her instincts flaring. She glanced around, noting the narrowing of the space between the two gates—

barely wide enough for a wagon to pass— and the tense stances of the knights now flanking her.

"What is the meaning of this?" she demanded, her voice sharp.

The lead knight stepped forward, his hand resting on the hilt of his sword. "By order of King Charon, you are hereby placed under arrest on charges of theft and treason."

Rubelle's heart sank, her grip tightening on the reins. "This is preposterous! I have served the royal family faithfully for years. On what grounds do you accuse me?"

The knight's expression was grim. "Direct orders, ma'am. King Charon himself."

"King Charon? You mean Prince..." She corrected as she noted the expression of the knights faulter for a moment before the one addressing her spoke up.

"You can prove your innocence after you've been brought before the **King**" He emphasized to which her heart sank. For Charon to be King that must have meant— 'No… this can't be!' she shook her head, her heart racing with more fear for her masters than herself. All of this was madness, but now she understood her Princess' reasons for sending her away even more. She could not allow herself to be captured.

This was no simple misunderstanding; Oriana's vision was already coming to pass.

"Mama, what's happening?" her daughter whispered, her voice trembling.

Rubelle forced a calm smile, though her insides churned. "It's nothing, my love. Just cover your ears for a moment."

The child hesitated but obeyed, burying her face in Rubelle's cloak.

Rubelle straightened, her eyes hardening as she turned back to the knights. "I have no quarrel with any of you. But I will not be caged like a criminal when my duty lies beyond these walls."

One of the knights reached for her reins. "Surrender now, and no harm will come to you or the child."

Rubelle's response was a burst of mythen so fierce that the air seemed to crackle. A glowing aura enveloped her as she raised a hand, and an explosion of raw energy erupted from her palm, slamming into the inner gate. The steel groaned and buckled under the force, the intricate carvings shattering as pieces of the wall crumbled.

The knights recoiled, their formations disrupted as shouts of alarm filled the narrow passage.

"Sound the horn! She's escaping!" one of them bellowed.

Rubelle seized the moment, urging her horse forward. The beast surged through the broken gate, leaping over the debris as the horns began to blare. Her daughter clung to her, her small fingers digging into Rubelle's sides as the horse bolted.

Behind them, chaos erupted. The knights scrambled to their horses, their armor clinking as they prepared to give chase. Rubelle didn't look back, her focus entirely on the road ahead.

The city's outskirts blurred past them as she pushed the horse to its limit. Her mind raced alongside her, the weight of the accusation and its implications bearing down on her. King Charon's direct involvement meant that any attempt to plead her case would be futile.

The horns grew fainter as they sped away from the walls, but Rubelle knew it was only a matter of time before the pursuit caught up to them. She was thankful they had not tried to shoot her or her horse down with arrows, but she knew they had to find a place to hide, to regroup, and to figure out how to protect her daughter— and the kingdom— from the shadow looming over them all.

As the walls faded into the horizon, Rubelle allowed herself one glance back. This task was proving to be much greater than she envisioned and now her heart sank at the possibility that she might not return to this place, to her family— to Therion.

"Mummy…" Dalia whimpered.

"Hold on tight," she murmured to her daughter, her voice both a promise and a plea.

And with that, they disappeared into the wilderness, the sound of hooves and horns fading into the night.

Chapter Five: Shadow of Death

Deep within the Shadowed Vale…

The combined armies' camp sprawled across the scorched plains, a grim testament to the battle's toll. Smoke rose in uneven columns, carrying the acrid stench of blood, charred flesh, and burning fur. The cries of the wounded mingled with the weary murmurs of soldiers tending to the living and the dead. Fires burned low in pits where the monstrous corpses were consigned, their grotesque shapes twisting into ash as their fangs, claws, and other useful materials had already been stripped. Yet the promise of profit from such trophies felt hollow against the immense loss they had suffered.

Therion stood near the edge of the camp, his broad shoulders weighed down by exhaustion.

His sharp gaze swept over the scene. Men moved like shadows, solemn and methodical, as they wrapped their fallen comrades in whatever cloth they could spare. A large, hastily erected tent served as the morgue, housing rows of bodies shrouded in stained linens.

The dead vastly outnumbered the living.

His frown deepened as his eyes lingered on the tent, its fabric sagging under the weight of grief. The surviving soldiers lacked the strength to bury their comrades properly; the thought of leaving them unburied was unbearable, but necessity offered no alternatives.

He let his gaze drift over the field of devastation, the churned earth still sticky with blood and strewn with fragments of shattered weapons. His mind turned toward the families waiting back home, blissfully unaware of the heartbreak barreling toward them. Therion clenched his fists, forcing himself to focus on the present. They were alive, but the question of what came next loomed large.

Near one of the burning pits, a group of soldiers worked tirelessly to ensure the monster corpses were fully destroyed. Some of the beasts had been massive, their twisted forms impossible to ignore even in death. The flames devoured them slowly, the stench of burning fur and sinew clinging to the air. One soldier paused, wiping sweat and soot from his brow, muttering a prayer under his breath.

Therion's attention returned to the dead within the tent. He couldn't help but wonder how Vaelrick, the late commander, would have handled this moment. He was vastly more experienced and would have probably rallied the men with an unflinching resolve. Though now he was nothing more than a headless corpse, leaving Therion to fill the void.

A dull throb in his forehead reminded him of his own injury— a jagged gash stitched together hastily in the chaos. It wasn't life-threatening, but the sting served as a bitter reminder of how close the battle had come to annihilation. He absently ran his fingers over the rough stitches, his thoughts distant. His wound could wait. There were too many who needed care far more desperately.

His musings were interrupted by the sight of Garrish limping toward him from across the camp. Even in the dim light, Therion could see the toll the fight had taken on him. Garrish was a mess— his armor dented and smeared with blood and dirt, a makeshift bandage tied clumsily around his head. Dark bruises bloomed across his face and arms, and his gait was unsteady. During the battle, one of the Hellspawn's cursed beams had flung him against a jagged rock. He'd been unconscious for most of the chaos, a small mercy considering the horrors they'd faced.

Therion stepped forward to meet him, his voice steady despite the turmoil around them. "How was it?"

Garrish didn't answer immediately. His expression was weary, his eyes haunted. Without a word, he handed Therion a battered piece of parchment.

Therion unfolded it carefully, scanning the grim report. The list of casualties was long— too long— and the names blurred together as a wave of nausea churned in his stomach. He clenched his jaw, forcing himself to focus. These were not just names; they were people— friends, fathers, brothers-in-arms.

"What now, sir?" Garrish's voice broke the heavy silence. It was low, hoarse, and filled with an exhaustion that ran deeper than physical fatigue.

Therion inhaled sharply, folding the parchment and tucking it into his belt. "Now, you get some rest. Tell the others to do the same. We've lost too much already; I won't lose anyone else to exhaustion."

Garrish hesitated, his brows knitting together. "You need rest too, Therion."

A faint, tired smile tugged at Therion's lips. "I'll rest. But not yet. Not until I've spoken with Lysara."

Garrish studied him for a moment, then nodded reluctantly. "Don't push yourself too far. We still need you."

"I'll keep that in mind," Therion replied, clapping a hand on Garrish's shoulder. He felt the tremor in the man's muscles, the weight of his battered spirit. "Go. Get some food and sleep. That's an order."

With another nod, Garrish turned and limped away, disappearing into the maze of tents and shadows.

Therion watched him go, his heart heavy.

Therion made his way toward the command tent, his boots crunching against the uneven ground. The night had grown colder, the chill biting against his skin through his worn armor. Around him, the camp stirred with subdued activity—murmured conversations, the occasional pained groan, and the distant crackle of a dying fire. The horrors of the battle clung to the air like a specter, and Therion felt its weight pressing on his shoulders with every step.

He stopped at the entrance to the command tent, the thick canvas flaps swaying slightly in the breeze. Taking a steadying breath, he cleared his throat and announced himself in a low, steady voice.

"Commander Lysara?"

Inside, Lysara was seated on a cot, her back straight despite the bandages wrapped tightly around her torso. Her healer worked diligently, sealing the last remnants of a grievous wound that had nearly claimed her life. Lysara's bare shoulders gleamed in the dim light of the lantern hanging overhead, her pale skin a stark contrast to the dark smudges of exhaustion beneath her eyes.

Therion froze, quickly averting his gaze at the sight of her exposed form. He stepped back, clearing his throat again as heat crept up his neck. "Apologies," he muttered.

Lysara glanced over her shoulder, her lips curving into a faint, tired smirk. "It's fine, Therion," she replied, her voice steady despite the weariness that laced it. "You're here because I sent for you anyway."

As the healer helped her into a modest robe, she turned to face him fully, her movements deliberate and restrained. The faint smirk lingered on her lips, though pain flickered behind her eyes. "Unless, of course, you find me distracting?" she teased lightly.

Therion huffed a dry laugh, shaking his head while keeping his gaze firmly fixed on hers. "Maybe I would have, if I didn't already have a wife."

That earned a soft, pained laugh from Lysara, though it ended in a harsh cough. She pressed a hand to her side as the healer scolded her under their breath. "Well, aren't you noble?" she murmured, though the humor didn't quite reach her eyes.

It didn't take a seasoned warrior to see that her strong front was a fragile façade. The wound in her abdomen had barely sealed, and even the healer's careful work couldn't mask the toll it had taken. The Hellspawn's attack had torn through her, leaving her pale as death and teetering on the edge of consciousness. She was alive now only by sheer willpower and the steady channeling of her mythen into her body.

"You shouldn't be sitting up," Therion said gently, stepping closer despite his earlier hesitation.

"Lying down isn't going to fix this mess," Lysara countered, grimacing as the healer dabbed at the edge of her bandages. She gestured weakly toward a nearby stool. "Sit."

Therion hesitated but complied, lowering himself onto the stool. His shoulders sagged under the weight of his thoughts, and his voice was heavy when he spoke. "We've lost too many."

"How many?" Lysara asked, her tone sharper than her weakened state suggested.

Therion paused, choosing his words carefully. "Of the two thousand Dracoseekers who marched here, only six hundred and fifty-four survived. Half of them are injured. My Emperor's Hand brought one thousand twenty knights. We suffered four hundred and three casualties." He hesitated, the next words catching in his throat. "And your Arcane Vanguard…" He trailed off, realizing his voice had taken on a mechanical tone, like a drone reciting grim statistics.

Lysara didn't press him for more. She already knew the cost had been staggering. The silence between them stretched, heavy and suffocating, before she finally spoke. "So… what now?"

"The injured alone will drain our supplies before we even reach the capital," Therion replied, running a hand through his unkempt hair. "And with the more experienced generals either dead or incapacitated…" He didn't finish the sentence. The enormity of their predicament hung unspoken in the air.

Lysara nodded slowly, her expression somber. "It's bad," she agreed. "But you're not here to talk about logistics, are you?"

Therion sighed, leaning forward and resting his elbows on his knees. His gaze dropped to the ground, his voice lowering. "It doesn't make sense. The Hellspawn… those monsters shouldn't have been able to summon something like that. Their mastery of mythen was crude at best. Someone more skilled must have been behind it."

Lysara exhaled slowly, her relief palpable. "I've been thinking the same thing," she admitted. "I've tried to contact the Knights Commander and our Monarchs, but there's been no response."

Therion's jaw tightened. "You want to tell them how the combined forces of their three strongest armies, nearly six thousand strong, were sent to the Shadowed Vale to terminate a Monster March half their number… only to be thwarted by a single abominable creature summoned from beyond the Veil?"

"They have to know," Lysara insisted.

"What if they already do?" Therion's voice was bitter. "What if they hoped we'd perish?"

Lysara opened her mouth to rebuke him, but the effort triggered another violent coughing fit, blood flecking her lips. The healer moved quickly, urging her to lie back. "That's enough for now, Commander," the healer said firmly, casting a pleading look at Therion. "She needs rest, not more of this."

Therion frowned but looked at Lysara, who weakly waved the healer off. "Therion," she rasped, her voice faint but resolute. "You've done more than enough for Orivera. Things would have been worse without you."

She reached for him, and as he stepped closer, her hand gripped his firmly. "I'll mirror the Knight Commander," she said, regaining some of her authority. "He needs to know what we've faced and the state of our armies."

Therion nodded, standing. "That's the best course of action. But please, Rest, Lysara."

Her lips twitched into a faint smile as she closed her eyes, the lines of tension in her face softening slightly. With a final glance at her, Therion stepped out of the tent. The cool night air greeted him like a slap, sharp and bracing against his skin.

The camp outside seemed even bleaker than before.

With nothing else to do he finally retired to his own tent. He was met by a merciful quiet that he appreciated as he sat heavily on his bed, his body aching in protest. He reached beneath his tunic, pulling out a small, battered locket. The hinge creaked as he opened it, revealing a tiny portrait of his wife and daughter. Their faces smiled up at him. Rubelle and Dalia were his world, and he found himself longing for them now more than ever.

With an exasperated sigh he cradled the locket against his chest and laid back, his eyes slipping shut as he murmured a quiet prayer. "Dear Goddess, please guide me back to them safely," he whispered, his voice trembling. Deep down, he felt it— a gnawing certainty that the worst was yet to come. What truly worried him was the wonder of how?

***

The night was eerily calm, the kind of stillness that wrapped around the camp like a shroud. The fires had burned low, their embers casting faint glows that flickered in the darkness. The air carried a serene chill, and for the first time in days, Therion allowed himself to sink into the quiet. Exhaustion claimed him quickly.

But serenity can be deceitful.

Therion jolted awake, his heart hammering against his ribs as his senses were assaulted all at once. The acrid stench of smoke clawed at his nostrils, and a distant roar shook the earth. His ears filled with a cacophony of chaos—shouting voices, the clash of steel, and a low, guttural growl that sent icy fingers down his spine.

He surged to his feet, instinct guiding him to his sword even as his mind struggled to piece together the nightmare unfolding outside. There was no time to don armor; his body moved before his thoughts could catch up.

The moment he stepped outside, the world turned into an inferno of chaos.

Tents were engulfed in roaring flames, their smoldering remains casting jagged shadows across the ground. Figures darted through the smoke—some armored, others barely dressed, all scrambling to survive. Horses reared and screamed, their terror a chilling harmony to the cries of dying men. One nearly trampled Therion, its eyes wide with panic as it bolted past.

He froze, his boots rooted to the ground, as his gaze swept the scene. There was no discernible order—just madness. A knight dashed by him, weapon drawn but with no clear direction, his face streaked with soot and terror. Somewhere in the distance, a tent collapsed with a deafening crash, flames licking hungrily at the night sky.

"Bandits?" Therion muttered aloud, though he knew the thought was absurd. No raider in their right mind would attack a force of this size, let alone with such precision.

The answer came in the form of a scream that cut through the night like a blade. Therion turned just in time to see a body hurled through the air, landing mere feet away from him with a sickening thud.

And then he saw it.

The creature was hunched low to the ground, moving with a predatory grace that made his blood run cold. Its grotesque form was barely illuminated by the firelight—a scaly, obsidian body that seemed to drink in the light. Six glowing red eyes lined the length of its elongated, serrated maw, each burning with a malevolent hunger.

It lunged forward, claws slicing through a knight with horrifying ease. Blood sprayed across the dirt as its tail, long and barbed like a scythe, lashed out and impaled another soldier mid-charge.

The creature's maw twisted into a mockery of a grin as it disemboweled its latest victim, dark ichor dripping from its jagged teeth.

Therion staggered back, his stomach churning.

"There's another?" he whispered, his voice barely audible over the din of battle.

Before he could process the nightmare before him, the earth erupted. A concussive blast tore through the camp, the shockwave sending Therion sprawling onto his back. His ears rang as he hit the ground hard, the breath knocked from his lungs.

He coughed violently, forcing himself upright as dirt and ash rained down around him. His sword was in his hand now, gripped so tightly that his knuckles ached.

Through the settling smoke, a new monstrosity emerged.

This one was even more imposing than the first. Its sinewy frame stretched unnaturally, covered in jagged, charred scales that glimmered like molten rock. Fire pulsed through its veins, visible beneath its translucent hide, and its eyes glowed like twin furnaces. A guttural snarl tore from its throat, reverberating through Therion's chest.

The beast reared its head, its maw opening impossibly wide. Fire spewed forth in a blazing arc, engulfing a group of fleeing soldiers. The explosion lit up the camp like a second sun, the screams of the dying muffled beneath the roar of flames.

Therion barely had time to react before another shape emerged from the haze. Then another. His heart clenched as he realized what he was seeing.

There were more of them.

Five Hellspawn. Each one a towering embodiment of destruction, their grotesque forms tearing through the camp like reapers of chaos.

A deep, primal fear took hold of him. They had struggled to defeat one earlier that day. Now there were five.

"Commander!"

The shout snapped Therion out of his stupor. He turned to see Garrish barreling toward him, his soot-streaked armor dented and cracked. Relief flashed across his friend's face, but it was fleeting.

"We have to go!" Garrish barked, grabbing Therion's arm with a grip born of desperation.

Therion hesitated for a heartbeat, his gaze flicking back to the carnage unfolding around them. His hand tightened around the hilt of his sword. He wanted to fight, to make a stand, but the rational part of his mind knew it would be suicide.

The Hellspawn were winning.

"Commander, now!" Garrish's voice was sharp, cutting through the roar of flames and the cries of the dying. "We have to go!"

Garrish managed to pull Therion along, their boots crunching against the dirt in uneven, hurried steps. Therion's body resisted every tug, his muscles taut with fury and a need for vengeance that clawed at his reason. Suddenly, a deafening thud resonated nearby— a Hellspawn landing. The ground beneath them seemed to shudder with its weight. Both men froze, their blood running cold as they turned toward the sound.

The monstrous creature loomed, its hulking, sinewy form barely visible through the haze of smoke and flickering firelight. Reflexively, Garrish yanked Therion toward the nearest cover—a pile of debris formed by the collapse of a supply wagon. The twisted frame of the wooden structure, partially blackened by fire, jutted upward at odd angles, its remnants forming a haphazard barricade. The acrid smoke from the burning supplies conccaled their position, curling around them like a poisonous veil.

They crouched low, Garrish pulling Therion close as the Hellspawn lumbered nearer. Its heavy, clawed feet crunched against the dirt, and its guttural snarl echoed ominously in the air. The creature paused mere fect from their hiding spot, its elongated snout twitching as it sniffed the air.

Therion's breath came in shallow gasps, not from fear but from the effort of containing his rage. His hand was white-knuckled against the hilt of his sword, trembling with the need to act. His jaw tightened as his glare bored into the creature, barely visible through the gaps in the debris.

Garrish's grip on his commander's arm tightened. He leaned closer, his voice a barely audible whisper. "You'll get yourself killed, sir."

But Garrish's words were meaningless against the tempest of fury roiling inside Therion. The cries of his dying men still echoed in his ears. The acrid stench of burning flesh, the grotesque sight of bodies torn apart—all of it fed the bitter storm in his mind. How could he sit and do nothing?

The Hellspawn took another step, its massive frame looming closer. Blood dripped from its claws and maw, the metallic tang mingling with the smoke and fire in the air. Garrish shot Therion a desperate glance, silently pleading with him not to give in to his anger.

And then, a sudden whistle cut through the chaos.

An arrow struck the Hellspawn in the shoulder, the impact burying the shaft deep into its scaly hide. The creature let out an earsplitting roar that reverberated through the camp, its glowing red eyes snapping to the source of the attack.

A lone knight stood defiantly in the distance, bow in hand and resolve etched into his soot-streaked face. He shouted something indistinct, his voice drowned out by the monster's rage.

With a furious snarl, the Hellspawn charged, its massive bulk plowing through what little remained of the camp as it barreled toward the knight.

"Now!" Garrish hissed, yanking Therion to his feet.

Therion staggered, caught off guard by the sudden movement. Garrish didn't wait for him to recover, pulling him forward with urgent strength.

They darted away from the wreckage, keeping low as they made for the tree line.

Therion's legs moved as if detached from his body, mechanically obeying Garrish's lead.

Suddenly, a sharp scream tore through the air behind them, snapping his attention back to the blazing remains of the camp. His heart seized as he saw them— the survivors who had rallied together amidst the carnage. Wounded men, barely able to stand, were defying the hellish beasts that had descended upon them. They stood in a ragged line, their weapons trembling in hands weakened by blood loss but steady with resolve.

"For O'Rivera! For Honor!" one of them roared, his voice hoarse but filled with unyielding defiance. The others echoed his cry, raising their enchanted blades high as they prepared for a final, hopeless stand.

Therion froze, his feet rooted to the ground. The sight of their bravery in the face of certain death was both inspiring and devastating. His chest heaved with emotion as he yanked his arm free from Garrish's grip.

"No!" Therion's voice cracked, raw with anguish. "My men—"

"It's too late for them," Garrish said, shame etched deep into his features.

Therion's voice rose, ragged and desperate. "We have to save them! We can't just watch them die!"

Garrish stepped in front of him, his hands gripping Therion's shoulders like iron. "They're already dead, sir! If we stay, we'll die too! Think of the others—think of Lysara. They need you."

Therion struggled against him, his eyes darting back to the camp where the hellspawns were converging on the remaining knights. The beasts moved with a cruel, deliberate intent, herding the survivors into a tight circle like predators playing with their prey. Then, in unison, the creatures unleashed their devastating fury.

Therion watched in horror as bursts of fire and dark energy engulfed the knights. The explosion lit up the night, and when the blinding light faded, nothing remained but a charred crater where his men had once stood. The banners they had so boldly clung to were gone, reduced to ash along with the brave souls who had held them.

The weight of his failure threatened to crush him. His legs buckled, and he sagged forward, his head hanging low as tears streamed down his face. "I swore to lead them," he whispered, his voice breaking. "I swore to protect them."

Garrish shook him, his own eyes glistening with unshed tears. "You think they'd want you to die here? To throw your life away for nothing? Dying here would dishonor them, Therion! We have to go now!"

Therion clenched his fists, his nails digging into his palms as he forced himself to stand upright. The grief and guilt were still there, clawing at him, but Garrish's words had struck a chord. He swallowed hard, his voice barely audible as he nodded. "You're right."

Seeing the resolve return to his friend's eyes, Garrish wasted no time. He led Therion through the dense forest, weaving between trees and bushes until they stumbled upon a burning supply wagon. The flames crackled fiercely, throwing flickering light across their desperate faces.

Suddenly, the sound of heavy footsteps echoed through the trees, accompanied by the guttural snarl of one of the hellspawns. The creature emerged from the shadows, its hulking form illuminated by the inferno. Its six glowing red eyes scanned the area, its claws digging into the earth as it sniffed the air.

Therion and Garrish ducked behind the wagon, their breaths shallow as they tried to remain silent. The creature's guttural growls grew louder as it prowled closer, the heat from the burning wagon scorching their skin. Therion gripped the hilt of his sword tightly, his knuckles white as he prepared to strike if the beast discovered them.

The hellspawn paused, its head snapping in their direction. Therion's heart thundered in his chest as he locked eyes with the monstrosity. Time seemed to freeze, the world narrowing to the space between him and the creature. Then, just as it began to move toward them, a sharp whistling sound cut through the air.

An arrow struck the hellspawn's flank, embedding itself in its thick hide. The beast let out a furious roar, its attention shifting to the knight who had fired the shot. The brave soldier stood a short distance away, his bowstring still vibrating as he nocked another arrow.

"Over here, you ugly bastard!" the knight shouted, his voice dripping with defiance.

The hellspawn turned away from the wagon, its predatory instincts honed on the new target. It charged after the knight, who fired another arrow before retreating into the forest. The distraction gave Therion and Garrish the precious seconds they needed.

"Move!" Garrish hissed, pulling Therion to his feet.

They ran, their boots pounding against the forest floor as the sounds of the hellspawn's pursuit faded behind them. Eventually, they reached a small stream where two horses stood tethered, their eyes wild with fear.

The animals stamped nervously as Garrish quickly untied them, his movements swift and practiced. "Mount up!" he urged, throwing himself onto his steed.

Therion hesitated, his gaze drifting back toward the camp. The flames were still visible through the trees, a blazing reminder of the lives lost. He clenched his jaw, forcing himself to look away as he mounted his horse.

Without another word, they spurred their mounts into a gallop, the forest blurring around them as they fled. The smell of smoke and blood lingered in the air, but Therion forced himself to focus on the path ahead.

"What happened back there?" Therion demanded at last, his voice shaking with fury and grief.

"Several of those hellspawns attacked out of nowhere," Garrish said grimly. "Commander

Lysara and the mages managed to lead a group of survivors into the mountains. But when I didn't see you, I knew I had to come back."

Therion glanced over his shoulder, his eyes narrowing as another explosion lit up the night sky. "They're hunting the survivors," he muttered, his voice filled with bitter realization.

Garrish nodded, his expression grim. "Ungodly things. We have to keep moving before they find our trail."

Therion urged his horse to go faster, the beast's hooves pounding against the dirt as they raced toward the mountains. Despite the fear gnawing at the edges of his mind, one thought burned brighter than all the rest: he had survived. By O'Rivera's grace, he had survived. But the night was far from over, and he swore he would not let it end in defeat.

Chapter Six: Nowhere to Hide

Dowry was a quiet, picturesque town nestled on the outskirts of the grand capital. Its cobblestone streets wove through modest homes with weathered shutters and gardens spilling over with bright flowers. The town was neither remarkable in size nor ambition, but its location as a natural stop for travelers heading toward the capital had kept it thriving for decades.

Merchants, adventurers, and pilgrims alike were drawn to its handful of bustling inns and taverns. The town boasted small marketplaces where one could procure fresh bread, dried meats, and trinkets from faraway lands. Dowry's residents had long perfected the art of hospitality, their livelihoods built upon the steady flow of travelers.

Most days, the town exuded a slow and contented rhythm. Farmers tended their fields on the outskirts, children played near the town square's ancient fountain, and the blacksmith's hammer rang out as it shaped tools and horseshoes for the next wave of visitors. The town's heart, however, lay in its inns, where laughter spilled out alongside the aroma of roasted meats and freshly poured ale.

Richman Walls' **The Lost Keg** was the crown jewel of Dowry's hospitality.

The inn, with its slanted roof and ivy creeping up its stone walls, was the largest and oldest establishment in town. Its hand-carved wooden sign swung on rusted hinges above the door, the 't' from 'Lost' conspicuously absent for years, a detail that had become an endearing quirk to locals and regular patrons alike.

Despite his advanced age, Richman still took pride in manning the counter himself. His daughter and her family frequently offered to take over, but he brushed off the suggestion with a hearty laugh, claiming that he'd retire 'when the sun stopped rising'. It was his life's work, a source of both pride and identity. The inn had seen countless travelers—tales of adventure, romance, and sorrow had played out in its halls. But even in all his years, nothing could have prepared Richman for the unprecedented disruption of that day.

It wasn't festival season, yet the streets of Dowry were packed with knights in gleaming armor marching in formation. They moved with purpose, boots thudding against the cobblestones, drawing wide-eyed stares from the townsfolk. Children were ushered indoors, merchants lowered their stall shutters, and an uneasy tension settled over the town like an oppressive fog.

At The Lost Keg, Richman was behind the counter when the door slammed open, and a cluster of knights strode in. Their leader, a broad-shouldered man with a commanding presence, stepped forward. His steely gaze swept across the room before settling on Richman.

"We're here on the king's orders," the knight said, his tone sharp. "A fugitive is believed to be hiding in this town. We'll need your full cooperation."

Richman's hand paused over the ledger he had been updating, his brow furrowing. Layla, his thirteen year old granddaughter, had been sweeping near the fireplace when the knights entered. She froze mid-motion, her knuckles white as she gripped the broomstick.

Richman waved her over with a steady hand, though his insides churned with unease. The presence of so many knights in his inn was far from ordinary. He had seen plenty of soldiers and adventurers pass through his doors, but this felt different— urgent, dangerous even.

"This is a modest establishment," Richman said carefully, his voice measured. "I can assure you, all my guests are law-abiding citizens."

The knight's eyes narrowed. "Regardless, we'll need to search the premises."

Richman hesitated. His years of experience had taught him that authority figures, especially those with power and weapons, were not to be antagonized lightly. He nodded slowly. "Of course. Though I only have two guests staying tonight— a young couple on their honeymoon down the hall and one of my regulars in the upstairs room. He's a scholar from Droggen."

He gestured to the ledger on the counter. "You're welcome to inspect the register if you'd like."

The knight dismissed the offer with a curt shake of his head. "Show us the rooms."

Richman's stomach tightened, though he kept his face neutral. He leaned down and whispered to Layla, "Stay here, child. Don't move until I return."

Her eyes darted between her grandfather and the imposing knights, but she nodded, clutching the broom as if it were a lifeline.

With a stiff gait, Richman led the knights down the dimly lit hallway.

The knights followed closely behind Richman as he shuffled down the narrow hallway of the inn. The wooden floor creaked beneath their armored boots, and the air was heavy with an unspoken tension. When they reached the first door, Richman knocked politely. There was no response.

He knocked again, a little firmer this time, but still, no one answered. Before he could try a third time, the lead knight stepped forward, raised his armored fist, and pounded on the door with a force that echoed down the hall.

"Knights from the Wall on official business! Open up!" the knight bellowed.

Moments later, the door creaked open, revealing a disheveled man leaning lazily against the frame. His hair was tousled, and water dripped from his bare chest as if he'd just stepped out of a bath. He regarded the knights with a smug, half-lidded gaze.

"To what do I owe the pleasure, good sirs?" he asked, his voice dripping with feigned politeness.

The lead knight explained their purpose brusquely, detailing their search for a fugitive rumored to be hiding in the town. Before he could finish, a woman's voice called from inside the room, soft and curious.

"Honey… who is it?"

The knight's gaze flicked over the man's shoulder to the dim interior, where a woman lay in bed, clutching the sheets tightly to her chest. The room smelled faintly of lavender and damp linen.

Satisfied that the couple was no threat, the knight cleared his throat and waved them off.

"There's no need to trouble yourselves further," he said gruffly.

The man's lips curled into a smirk as he shut the door, locking it with a soft click that seemed louder than it should have in the tense silence.

Richman exhaled slowly and gestured back toward the staircase. "The other room is upstairs," he said, his voice steady despite the tightness in his chest.

The lead knight narrowed his eyes beneath his helmet, casting a suspicious glance around the hallway. "How many rooms are available in this inn?"

"Twelve in total," Richman answered without hesitation, the practiced reply rolling off his tongue.

The knight paused, calculating something in his head. "And how much do you charge for a night?"

Richman quoted the standard rate, watching as the knight exchanged a glance with one of his companions. The latter nodded curtly and turned to leave.

"Inform the others that we'll be staying here tonight after we've combed through the other establishments," the knight instructed. "It's possible the fugitives have already passed through town, but we'll ensure no stone is left unturned."

"Yes, sir," the subordinate replied, marching off to relay the message.

The lead knight turned back to Richman, his voice losing some of its edge. "How soon can you have a meal prepared for six men?"

Richman's practiced smile never faltered. "Give me twenty minutes, sir, and it'll be ready. What would you like?"

"Anything but cold oatmeal," the knight muttered, removing his helmet to reveal a weary, sweat-slicked face. "And ale. Plenty of ale. Our horses will be tethered outside."

"Of course," Richman said with a bow, already mentally preparing the meal. "If you'll follow me, I'll show you the rooms you'll be staying in."

A short while later...

The other knights arrived, just as the lead knight had said. Once inside the inn's modest walls, they allowed themselves to relax. The tension from their relentless pursuit began to melt away as they removed their helmets and shrugged off their heavy cloaks. They exchanged quiet grumbles and tired jokes, their exhaustion evident in the way they slumped into chairs and stretched their aching limbs.

Richman, ever the diligent host, ensured their needs were met with efficiency and care. Once the knights were occupied with their food and ale, he returned to the counter, where his granddaughter, Layla, waited with wide, curious eyes.

"Do you think they're looking for Auntie Belle?" she whispered, her voice barely audible.

Richman's heart skipped a beat, but he kept his expression calm. He pressed a finger to his lips and gently covered her mouth with his hand, glancing around to ensure no one had overheard.

"Don't you worry about that, darling," he said softly, flashing her a reassuring smile. "Just do as I say, and I promise you a dessert before dinner."

Layla's eyes lit up at the promise, and she nodded eagerly before darting outside to tend to the knights' horses as instructed.

Richman watched her go, his smile fading as soon as she was out of sight. He moved quickly then, reaching beneath the counter to retrieve a small, tarnished key. It fit the lock to a hidden door at the back of the inn, a door that most visitors never even noticed.

The door creaked open, revealing a narrow staircase that descended into the inn's cellar. It was a small space, crammed with barrels of ale and sacks of grain, but in one shadowed corner stood a cot draped in thick blankets.

There, a woman sat on the edge of the cot, her face lined with worry as she stroked the hair of a sleeping child beside her.

"Rubelle," Richman whispered, stepping into the room and shutting the door behind him.

"They came, just like you said they would," Richie announced as he stepped into the room.

Rubelle gave him a stern look, and he quickly waved his hand, realizing what worried her. "No need to fret," he assured her. "The walls are thick here. I even added a layer of foam. No sound gets in— or out."

His modifications, originally meant to block the noise of unruly guests, now served as a safeguard for their secret.

"Thank you, Sir Richie. I don't know how I could ever repay you," Rubelle said softly.

"Nonsense, child," Richie replied, shaking his head as he grabbed a stool and pulled it closer to her. "You're practically a daughter to me. How could I refuse you?"

Her lips curled into a small smile, touched by his unwavering kindness. For a moment, memories stirred—some warm, others shadowed by pain.

Rubelle had no recollection of her parents. Her earliest memories were of the dingy cage she was shoved into by the savages who had razed her home village. It was Prince Charon who had rescued her from that nightmare. However, he didn't have the time to care for her personally. Instead, he had brought her to this very inn, paying its owner handsomely to care for her until she recovered from her ordeal.

Richie had done far more than what was asked. Months turned into years, and he became not just her caretaker but a true father figure. Rubelle, who was close in age to Richie's daughter, Lilian, grew up feeling like part of his family. He treated the two girls like sisters, offering Rubelle a sense of belonging she had thought lost forever.

Had Richie not taken her in, Rubelle doubted her life would have turned out the way it did.

"So, this is your little Dalia," Richie said, his voice warm as he beamed at the sleeping child.

Rubelle's smile widened as she nodded, quietly sharing Dalia's age. Richie chuckled, his joy evident.

"I can't believe I've finally gotten the chance to meet her," he said, his gaze lingering fondly on the child. Rubelle had often told him stories about Dalia during her visits to the inn, but this was the first time she had brought her daughter along.

Yet as Richie turned his attention back to Rubelle, he noticed the worry etched into her face. His heart ached with regret, wishing this visit could have been under better circumstances— a holiday, perhaps, rather than a desperate escape.

"She's beautiful," Richie said softly, trying to lighten the moment. "You've done well, Rubelle."

"Thank you," she murmured, brushing a hand over Dalia's dark curls.

Richie sighed, leaning back on his stool. "I only wish you didn't have to be here under such a cloud. But don't you worry, my girl. You're safe here. No one will find you."

Rubelle nodded, her gratitude unspoken but clear in her eyes.

Despite that, He couldn't help but notice the worry also etched across her face. It made his heart ached at the sight. Taking her hands in his own, he gave them a gentle squeeze. Her hands were warm, soft, and much larger now, a stark contrast to the tiny hands he used to hold when she was just a child. Back then, her hands fit perfectly in his palm, delicate and fragile. Time had changed her— grown her into a strong, capable woman— but to him, she would always be the little girl he had taken in all those years ago.

Looking into her eyes, he offered her the same reassuring smile he had given countless times before. "I'm sure this is all just a misunderstanding," he said with a calm certainty that almost made her believe it. "The truth will come out, and I bet this will all blow over before you know it."

Rubelle swallowed the lump in her throat, desperate to let his words soothe her frayed nerves. Oh, how she wanted to believe him— to accept his optimism as truth. But the horrible waves of energy that had washed over them earlier still lingered in her mind, a grim reminder of the reality they faced. This wasn't the kind of trouble that simply blew over. It was something far darker, far more dangerous than he could imagine.

Still, she managed a small smile, forcing herself to find strength in his presence. "Dalia and I have been riding all day," she said softly, her voice tinged with weariness. "We're famished."

He chuckled, a warm, familiar sound that briefly eased her worries. "Then let me fix that," he said, patting her hand one last time before rising from his chair. "I'll get some food. You two rest up."

With that, he turned and left the room, his figure retreating up the wooden steps and out with the gentle thud of its door shutting.

Left alone, Rubelle exhaled deeply, her shoulders sagging as the weight of their situation pressed down on her. Her gaze shifted to her daughter, who lay curled up on the makeshift bed, her chest rising and falling in the deep rhythm of sleep. Rubelle leaned over, brushing a stray lock of hair from Dalia's face.

"I'll keep you safe," she whispered, her voice barely audible. Stroking her daughter's soft curls, she pressed a gentle kiss to her forehead.

The decision settled firmly in her mind. This was the safest place for Dalia to stay— at least for now. Richman would understand. She would talk to him in the morning, lay out her plan, and ensure her daughter remained protected.

But for now, her stomach growled, reminding her that it had been far too long since she'd eaten. By the time Dalia woke, she would undoubtedly be hungry too. Rubelle stood quietly, her resolve solidifying. Protecting Dalia was her priority, but first, she needed to replenish her strength for whatever came next.

Later that night…

Mr. Richie had collected the plates from the meal he served and Rubelle was sure he would not return until morning, likewise Dalia felt right asleep once her belly was full. The poor girl was clearly far more exhausted than her mother, and yet Rubelle couldn't bring herself to sleep. She'd climbed in bed beside her daughter but finally let out a long, steady breath. Getting out of bed she moved over to the other end of the room. She knew what was gnawing away at her, and she knew answers were the only thing that would allow her mind to rest. She decide to attempt a mirroring.

Her back sank against the wall, and she crossed her legs, sitting on the cold, earthen floor.

She glanced over at Dalia, who remained peacefully asleep, her small hands curled into fists as though she had no worries in the world. Rubelle envied her daughter's innocence but knew she couldn't afford to rest until her own mind was eased.

The princess.

Rubelle's thoughts turned to Oriana, the young woman she had sworn to protect with her life. She needed to know if Oriana was safe. Without that assurance, Rubelle feared she would never find peace.

Closing her eyes, she began to steady her breathing, a rhythm that drew her focus inward. She stilled her thoughts, reaching deep into the well of energy that was her connection to the mythen. Around her, the mythen began to stir, faint threads of light shimmering in the dim room.

Rubelle extended her palms before her, feeling the warmth of the energy as it coalesced in the air. The process was painstaking, requiring delicate concentration. Her breaths grew deeper, her chest rising and falling as she guided the threads, weaving them together like strands of silk.

The mythen began to form a shape— a solid, circular disc hovering above her hands. It shimmered faintly at first, translucent and formless, but as she continued, the threads thickened, condensing into a surface that gleamed with a faint silver hue. Slowly, painstakingly, the shimmering surface became smooth and reflective.

The base for her spell was ready: a mirror crafted from pure mythen.

But that was the easy part.

Rubelle opened her eyes, staring into the gleaming disc before her. The reflection was faint, like a pond rippling with unseen currents. She reached out with her mind, thinking of Oriana— her image, her voice, her very essence. Rubelle's thoughts spiraled outward, beckoning to the princess across the vast distance that separated them.

The mirror began to hum softly, its surface swirling as it sought to connect with the Princess' *Contact Mirror* in the castle.

At the castle, Oriana stirred in her bed, a shiver running down her spine. She sat up, her hand instinctively moving to the dagger beneath her pillow. Her mind raced, disoriented. *Why am I still here?* She wondered as she glanced around the familiar confines of her chamber, disbelief washing over her. After everything that had happened, she had not expected to wake here.

Her confusion deepened as she noticed a faint glow emanating from her lower drawer. Her heart quickened. There was only one person that knew she owned a personal contact mirror and she needed to hear from them just as urgently as they sought to hear from her. Slipping out of bed,

Oriana rushed to the drawer, pulling it open to reveal the small, reflective glass. Its edges lined with gems and runes as the surface shimmered and pulsed with ethereal light as it came alive when she said the words. 'I am listening,'

"Rubelle?" she whispered the instant their mirrors connection was established, cradling the mirror in her hands. The light coalesced into the familiar face of her friend. Relief flooded through Oriana as Rubelle's image came into focus, her warm smile a balm to both their frayed nerves.

"Thank the Goddess, you're alive!" Rubelle breathed. "When I heard Charon had taken the throne. I didn't know what to expect."

Oriana nodded, her voice trembling. "It's a miracle, really. But Rubelle… did you make it beyond the Wall?"

"I did," Rubelle replied quickly, her voice steady. "We're safe, but we didn't make it far from the capital. Oriana, what's going on? Why are the knights after me?"

Oriana hesitated, guilt flashing across her face. "I'm sorry, Rubelle. I never meant to endanger you. It's Charon— he gave the order."

"Charon?" Rubelle repeated, her brow furrowing. "Why would the Monarchs allow him to do such a thing?"

Oriana's expression darkened, her voice dropping to a near whisper. "Because there *are* no Monarchs."

Rubelle stared at her, stunned. "What do you mean?"

"Charon killed them," Oriana said flatly, her voice laced with grief. "Our parents. He… he murdered them, Rubelle. And it's only a matter of time of time before I'm next."

Rubelle's stomach twisted in disbelief. She opened her mouth to respond, but a chill ran through her as Oriana continued.

"There's more," Oriana said, her voice shaking. "Something darker is at play. Charon's allied himself with the—"

Suddenly, Oriana froze, her eyes widening into a terrifying deformed face that sent a chill down Rubelle's spine. But the princess was fine, Rubelle could quickly tell that something else was tempering with her spell. Suddenly, a cold, malevolent energy seeped through the connection. Voices, low and guttural, began to mutter over and over again all around her.

Found you… you can't hide… found you…

Rubelle's breath hitched. She clutched her hands tightly, trying to stabilize the mirror, but the voices grew louder, more insistent.

"No!" Rubelle shouted, pouring too much of her energy into the spell out of fear. The mirror shook, the voices seeping into her mind like venom. They laughed, a sinister chorus echoing through her thoughts. With a cry, Rubelle released the spell, sending a powerful jolt of magic outward. The force rattled the walls of the hidden chamber, and the mirror she had crafted shattered into fragments of light.

Oriana wasn't unscathed either.

She gasped as her own mirror flew from her hands, landing on the floor with a resounding crash. The shards scattered, their glow fading as the malevolent voices erupted into mocking laughter.

"No!" Oriana screamed, covering her ears. "Leave me alone!"

The voices subsided as suddenly as they had come, leaving her alone in the suffocating silence of her room. She hugged her knees, her breath coming out in ragged huffs. "Goddess," she whispered, her voice trembling. "Protect her. Protect Rubelle for me."

Tears streamed down her face as she stared at the broken shards on the floor, her heart heavy with fear. She had no doubt the malevolent force had found her friend.

And she prayed it wasn't too late.

***

It was a long night, but dawn came in due time…

Richman stood at the desk, absently tapping his fingers on the worn wood as the knights from the previous night approached. Their faces were calm, even friendly, as they handed over the coins for their stay.

"Thank you for the meal, innkeeper," one of them said, nodding with genuine appreciation.

Richman forced a smile, his genial innkeeper persona firmly in place. "Of course. You're welcome back anytime."

The knights offered polite farewells before stepping out into the morning light. Richman followed them to the door, his expression tight as he waited for them to disappear down the road. Only once they were out of sight did he allow his mask to slip. He closed the door carefully, then immediately turned and kicked a hidden latch near the base of the wall. A faint click echoed through the room as a concealed door swung open.

"Alright, out you come," he called softly, motioning into the secret chamber.

Rubelle emerged first, her movements tense and deliberate, followed by Dalia, who clung to her mother's hand.

"The knights are gone," Richman said, ushering them into the main room. "But don't go just yet. Give it a moment to make sure the coast is clear."

Rubelle nodded, her face pale as she took in the quiet inn. Despite her attempts to appear calm, Richman noticed the way her hands trembled slightly.

"You don't look well," he said, his brow furrowing. "If you're sick, you can't travel like this."

"I'm fine," Rubelle insisted, waving off his concern.

Richman opened his mouth to argue, but the conversation was interrupted by a sudden knock at the door. Rubelle's eyes widened, and without a word, she grabbed Dalia and ducked behind the counter. Richman shot them a warning glance to stay quiet as he strode toward the door. He cracked it open just enough to peek outside, his tension melting into surprise when he saw who it was.

"Lilian?" he asked, stepping back to allow his daughter in.

Lilian pushed her way inside, her expression impatient. "Good morning to you too, Father. And before you say it, I know I wasn't supposed to be here until later, but I heard Rubelle was around, so I came to see her."

Richman scowled, glancing nervously toward the counter. "Lilian, this isn't the time for—"

"Rubelle!" Lilian exclaimed, spotting her half-sister as Rubelle hesitantly rose from her hiding spot.

Before Richman could stop her, Lilian darted forward, throwing her arms around Rubelle in a tight embrace. "It's been so long! I can't believe you're here."

Rubelle returned the hug with a small smile, her usual warmth tempered by the weight of her current predicament.

When Lilian noticed Dalia peeking shyly from behind her mother, her face lit up. "And this must be your little one!" she said, crouching down to Dalia's level. "Hello there. Aren't you adorable?"

Rubelle's smile softened as she watched Lilian interact with Dalia, but there was a flicker of something else in her eyes— worry, or perhaps hesitation.

"Come on," Lilian urged, straightening up. "Let's sit down and catch up properly."

Richman stepped in, his tone firm. "We don't have time for that. They were just about to leave."

But Rubelle shook her head, placing a hand on his arm. "It's alright. We'll wait a little longer."

Richman muttered something under his breath, clearly unhappy, but relented. "Fine," he said, heading toward the kitchen. "I'll make breakfast then. Might as well eat something before you go."

Rubelle, Lilian, and Dalia moved to the small table in the living area, settling into the mismatched chairs. Lilian began chatting animatedly, recounting her recent travels and asking questions about Rubelle's life and Dalia's upbringing.

Though Rubelle nodded and answered where she could, her mind seemed elsewhere. Her gaze kept flicking toward the windows and doors, her body taut with unease.

Rubelle took a deep breath and knelt beside Dalia. "Why don't you go help Grandpa Richie in the kitchen, sweetheart?" she said, her voice soft but steady. "He might need an extra hand with breakfast."

Dalia hesitated, her wide eyes searching her mother's face for reassurance. Rubelle smiled gently and brushed a lock of hair from her daughter's forehead. "Go on. I'll call you when we're ready to eat."

Reluctantly, Dalia nodded and padded off to the kitchen. Lilian watched her go with a wistful sigh, leaning back in her chair. "They grow up so fast," she murmured dreamily. "It feels like just yesterday you were the one running around with messy hair and scraped knees."

Rubelle thought it was funny, Lilian had just described her younger self. Rubelle was rather quiet and reserved as a child, in fact the two of them were a grave contrast from each other, but they got along so well. She smiled at Lilian, it'd actually been awhile since she'd seen her. "Last I heard you were pregnant."

"It was a boy this time." Lilian boasted with her head high, "And he will be my last. Three kids are a lot of work."

Rubelle nodded, "Congratulations."

"I should be congratulating you. While I played the perfect housewife, you were busy moving up in the world. Miss Court Mage." She teased though her word didn't receive the reaction she'd hoped. Rubelle sighed, palming her face.

"You didn't hear. I got demoted to fugitive."

She frowned. "I noticed," Lilian glanced about out of habit as if checking to be sure they were alone before she leaned forward with her chin resting on her palms. "What kind of trouble have you gotten yourself into this time?"

"The kind of trouble that'd get you into trouble if I told you about it."

"Does it have something to do with those awful energy surges yesterday?" Lilian perked up, and although Rubelle did not respond, her silence spoke volumes. "That's awful."

"Lilian…" Rubelle started strongly doing away with the passive small talk they had going for something she'd been thinking of for a while, "I wasn't expecting to see you today… but I'm glad you came. I need a favor."

"Anything," Lilian responded sharply without a moment's hesitation. "Anything at all. Just ask."

Rubelle drew in a shaky breath, her eyes meeting her sister's. "I need you to take care of Dalia."

Lilian blinked, the words taking a moment to sink in. "Come again."

"I want to leave Dalia here. With you." Rubelle stole a glance at her daughter in the kitchen. Smiling and being ever so cheerful as she helped the old man beat some eggs— that smile was precious and she feared she might not be able to protect it on her own. The ominous power that attacked her last night had made it clear that whatever was after the key was far more dangerous than simply armed men. "She can't come with me. This task… where am heading… it's too dangerous for a child."

Lilian's expression mirrored her sisters, she could see this was a difficult choice for her to make and she had no qualms with being of service, but there was a bigger matter to address. "I understand how you feel, but does Dalia know about this? Are you sure that's what *she* wants? What you really want."

Rubelle shook her head. She didn't want to leave her daughter, she didn't care how perilous the journey was. But it didn't matter what she wanted. "She doesn't understand what's happening, and I don't want her to. I just know I can't trust anyone else to keep her safe."

"Rubelle—"

Her voice cracked as she reached for Lilian's hand, interrupting her. "Please. You're the only one I can ask."

For a moment, Lilian seemed torn, her gaze flickering between her sister's pleading face and the kitchen where Dalia and her father were pleasantly unaware of their conversation. Finally, she placed her other hand over Rubelle's and squeezed gently.

"I'll take care of her," she promised. "But only if you promise to come back safely. She needs her mother, Rubelle. Don't let her grow up without you."

Rubelle opened her mouth to respond, but her attention was caught by something in the corner of her eye— a shadow that didn't belong. It slithered unnaturally along the floor, dark and menacing, yet cast by nothing visible as a voice too close for comfort whispered.

Found you…

Her breath caught in her throat as icy fear gripped her. Without thinking, she bolted upright, knocking her chair over in the process as mythen flared about her body in a dull golden aura.

Lilian jumped, startled by her sister's sudden movement. "Rubelle, what's wrong?"

Rubelle scanned the room, but the shadow was gone as quickly as it had appeared. But it was there, that wasn't a hallucination. She shook her head, trying to calm her racing heart as Lilian grabbed her wrist. "Rubelle… you're scaring me."

Her sister's eyes were panicked and struck her with guilt as she releasing the aura about her, calming as she apologized. "What happened?" Lilian pressed, her concern growing.

"I don't know," Rubelle lied, her voice trembling. She recognized the presence. It was the same darkness from last night. She clutched her arms tightly, as if warding off the lingering chill.

Lilian frowned. "Are you sure you're not just exhausted? You've been through a lot."

Rubelle shook her head more firmly this time. Rest was tempting but she knew better, whatever it was, it'd found her and that meant this place wasn't safe. Not for her or Dalia— but she hoped leaving would at least make it safe for Lilian and her own family. "No... I'm sorry. We have to go."

"Wait... what?"

Ignoring Lilian she turned abruptly toward the kitchen doorway and called out, "Dalia! We're leaving!"

"Already? I was just about to Richman and Dalia emerged from the kitchen, both looking confused and concerned. Lilian was equally taken aback. "Rubelle, wait—"

"I can't risk it," Rubelle said, her voice resolute. She pulled Dalia into a tight embrace. "You're safer with me."

Lilian placed a hand on her sister's shoulder, searching her face. "But you just said—"

"It doesn't matter," Rubelle interrupted, her tone softening as she met Lilian's bewildered gaze.

"Thank you, but I can't leave her behind. Not now."

Lilian hesitated, clearly wanting to argue but recognizing the determination in her sister's eyes. Instead, she sighed. "At least let us pack something for the road. You can't leave without food or supplies."

Rubelle nodded reluctantly. "Fine. But only for a moment."

As Lilian and Richman hurried to gather provisions, Dalia clung to her mother's side, her small face scrunched with worry. "Are we in trouble, Mama?" she whispered.

Rubelle crouched down and held her daughter close, her heart aching at the fear in her voice. "No, sweet girl," she murmured, kissing Dalia's forehead. "I won't let anything hurt you. I promise."

Dalia's gaze searched her mother's face, and though she didn't fully understand the danger, she nodded, trusting Rubelle's words.

Within minutes, Lilian and Richman returned with a small satchel of food and a bundle of warm blankets. "Take this," Lilian said, handing the bag to Rubelle. "And... take care of yourself, alright?"

Rubelle nodded, pulling her sister into a brief but heartfelt hug. "Thank you," she whispered.

As they snuck out the front with their hoods over their heads as they made their way to their horse in a hurry.

Chapter Seven: The Bridge

The Frozen Peaks loomed over the shadowed vale like jagged teeth, their icy edges glinting in the pale sunlight. The air was thin, biting with every breath, and the peaks seemed to stretch endlessly into a canvas of grey and blue. Snow cascaded from precariously perched overhangs, and frost clung to the rough stone surfaces, making the path treacherous even for the most experienced riders. The wind howled through the narrow passes, a haunting symphony that seemed to mock their fragile warmth.

Therion clung to his reins, his fingers numb despite his gloves. His cloak, though thick, was woefully inadequate against the bitter cold that seemed to seep into his very bones. Garrish, riding beside him, fared no better, his armor rimed with frost. Each exhalation formed a thin cloud that dissipated almost as quickly as it appeared.

From the opposite ridge, Lysara rode toward them, her steed's hooves crunching against the hardened snow. A dull shimmer of mythen surrounded her, radiating faint warmth that cut through the biting cold like a fragile shield. The spell spread outward as she approached, easing the relentless chill for the group.

"We can't take the main roads," she said as she reached them, her voice firm but edged with exhaustion. "Those hellspawn will be patrolling the routes out of the vale. These mountains are the only way."

Therion scanned their surroundings with a grim expression. The peaks were treacherous and unforgiving, the paths narrow and crumbling. Sheer drops yawned beside them, plunging into shadowy depths that seemed bottomless. The mountain paths were littered with loose rocks hidden beneath a thin layer of snow, ready to betray an unwary step.

No sane person would dare to scale these heights—only desperation could drive someone here.

"We're lucky there's no storm," Garrish muttered, his teeth chattering. "If the wind picked up, we'd be done for."

Therion didn't respond, his gaze falling on the small cluster of riders ahead. Seven others. That was all that remained of their once-proud force. His chest tightened as he spurred his mount forward.

"Is this all that's left of us?" he asked, his voice low.

Lysara pulled her horse to a halt and turned to face him. Her lips pressed into a thin line before she spoke. "We underestimated the hellspawn. Nothing could have prepared us for the ambush."

Therion's frown deepened. "Where did they come from?"

"The veil," Garrish interjected grimly, his eyes fixed ahead.

Both Lysara and Therion turned to him, but Garrish didn't flinch under their scrutiny.

"The second wave of mythen we felt yesterday," he continued. "If the first came from the rift, then surely the rest must have come from another." He paused, his voice heavy with regret. "We were too battered after the first battle to think of it."

Lysara exhaled sharply, her breath visible in the frigid air. "Speculating about their origin won't help us now," she said. "What matters is that we keep moving. We need to reach the peak before the warmth spell wears off."

Therion frowned. "And then what? How are we supposed to return to the capital? The only way down is through the mountain paths."

Lysara's expression darkened, but she didn't meet his eyes. "We're not going to the capital," she said curtly, turning her horse and rallying the others. "Keep moving!"

Therion exchanged a puzzled glance with Garrish before urging his horse forward, catching up to Lysara. "What do you mean we're not going to the capital?" he pressed in a low voice.

Lysara hesitated, glancing at the others to ensure they weren't listening. She leaned closer to Therion and whispered, "Something terrible has happened. Charon has claimed the throne."

Therion's heart sank, his breath catching in his throat.

"No," he whispered, the word barely audible.

The pieces of the puzzle began to fall into place, each one more damning than the last. Their oaths bound them to their monarchs— not just in loyalty, but through a sacred authority that compelled their very souls. It was an honor that set them apart from ordinary knights, a bond that granted them strength and purpose.

But now, that same oath had marked them for death.

With the king and queen dead, Charon must have sought to destroy them, fearing their loyalty would drive them to vengeance. Therion stared up at the vast expanse of grey, blue, and white, his mind reeling. Betrayal stung sharper than the mountain wind, its weight pressing down on him like the icy peaks themselves.

"I don't believe it," he muttered, his voice trembling.

Lysara's expression softened, but there was no comfort in her eyes. "We have no choice now," she said quietly. "If we return to the capital, we're walking into a death trap. Charon won't allow us to live."

Therion's gaze dropped to the path ahead, his jaw tightening. "Then where are we going?"

"I have a plan," Lysara said. "I just pray we live long enough to see it through."

Behind them, Garrish called out, his voice cutting through the silence. "Careful! The path ahead is narrow."

The group slowed as they approached a particularly treacherous stretch of the trail. The ground beneath their horses' hooves was uneven, the snow masking jagged rocks and hidden crevices. To their right, the cliff dropped into an abyss, the depths swallowed by shadow.

Lysara dismounted and led her horse by the reins, motioning for the others to do the same.

"Stay close and move carefully," she instructed. "One misstep and—"

The ground beneath her foot gave way with a sickening crunch. She stumbled, her hands scrabbling for purchase, but Garrish lunged forward and grabbed her arm, pulling her back to solid ground.

"Watch your step," he said, his voice rough with exertion.

Lysara nodded, her face pale. "That's what await…." She clarified with a terrifying certainty.

Therion took a deep breath, his grip on the reins tightening. His men got the message, and thankfully none of them were unfortunate. The weight of their predicament pressed heavily on Therion, but he couldn't afford to falter. Not now.

As they continued their ascent, the distant peak came into view, its silhouette stark against the overcast sky. It seemed impossibly far, but it was their only hope.

Therion's thoughts churned as he trudged forward, his mind replaying Lysara's words. The betrayal, the danger, the uncertainty— it all swirled together in a storm of doubt and rage. But as he glanced back at the survivors following in their wake, he knew they couldn't afford to dwell on what they'd lost. Their focus had to be on what lay ahead— on the slim chance of survival that awaited them beyond these Frozen Peaks.

The snow began to fall harder, thick and relentless, until all they could see was an endless expanse of grey. Whether it was day or night was anyone's guess; the sun was a distant memory, its feeble light swallowed by the storm. The cold seeped into their bones despite the faint warmth emanating from the mages' mythen, the spell's glow flickering like a dying ember.

Therion tightened his cloak around his shoulders, his jaw clenched against the bitter chill. The soldiers murmured to one another, their voices heavy with unease. The snowfall was so dense it blurred the path ahead, and their horses struggled to find footing on the ice-slicked trail. One by one, the riders dismounted, leading their mounts carefully forward as the terrain grew too treacherous to navigate on horseback.

Garrish pulled his reins close, walking beside Therion as they trudged through the snow. His breath formed pale clouds in the frigid air, his voice low. "Do you know where Lysara's taking us?"

Therion glanced ahead, where Lysara led the group, her figure nearly swallowed by the storm. She moved with purpose, but even from a distance, Therion could see the strain in her movements. The faint light of the mythen illuminated her face, revealing lines of pain and exhaustion etched deep into her features.

"She's in no better shape than the rest of us," Garrish muttered, shaking his head.

Therion frowned, his eyes lingering on Lysara. Despite her injuries, there was a fire in her gaze, a fierce determination that refused to be extinguished. "She knows what she's doing," he said finally.

Garrish nodded, though his expression remained uncertain. He opened his mouth to speak again but stopped abruptly, his head snapping to the side at the sound of a muffled cry.

One of the knights had collapsed, his body crumpling into the snow. Garrish cursed under his breath, rushing to the fallen soldier. The others stopped, their faces pale as they gathered around.

"He's out cold," Garrish said grimly, his hands on the knight's shoulders.

Lysara turned at the commotion, her gaze narrowing as she scanned the group. Her lips tightened when she saw the man on the ground. "There's a cave ahead," she said, pointing toward a dark shadow barely visible through the snow. "We'll rest there."

The group moved quickly, the promise of shelter lending them strength. The cave loomed larger as they approached, its wide mouth yawning open like a maw in the mountainside. The entrance was partially obscured by snow, but once inside, the space opened into a massive cavern.

The walls glistened with frost, and icicles hung like jagged teeth from the ceiling. The ground was uneven, with patches of bare stone peeking through the snow. Faint streams of water trickled down the walls, glimmering faintly in the dim light of their mythen. The cavern extended deeper into the mountain, the shadows swallowing whatever lay beyond.

"Get him inside," Lysara ordered, her tone clipped but not unkind.

The soldiers carried the unconscious knight into the cavern, laying him near one of the walls. The others quickly began gathering what little firewood they had left, building a makeshift fire in the center of the space. Lysara stood at the entrance, her hands outstretched as she muttered an incantation.

A thin veil of protection shimmered to life, an illusionary mythen spreading across the mouth of the cave. From within, they could see the edges of the spell, a faint line where the cave ended, and the illusion began. But from the outside, the cave was invisible, the veil blending seamlessly with the snow-covered mountainside.

Lysara lowered her hands with a soft sigh, turning back to the group. The men were huddled around the fire, their faces illuminated by the flickering flames. The warmth was faint but welcome, the glow chasing away some of the chill that clung to their bodies.

Therion stood near the fire, his arms crossed as he watched the others. Lysara approached him, her steps slow and measured. She rubbed her hands together, trying to coax warmth back into her fingers.

"We're lucky we found this place," she said quietly, her voice barely audible over the crackle of the fire.

Therion glanced at her, his brow furrowed. "How long do you think we can stay here?"

"Not long," Lysara admitted. "The storm will pass, but it won't take the hellspawn long to realize we've left the main roads. They'll start searching the mountains soon enough."

Therion nodded grimly, his gaze drifting to the unconscious knight. "And him? Will he make it?"

Lysara's expression softened, but she didn't answer right away. She crouched beside the fire, holding her hands over the flames. "He'll need rest, and so will the rest of us. We can't afford to lose anyone else."

Therion crouched beside her, his voice dropping to a whisper. "Where are we going really, Lysara? If not the capital, then where else could we be safe?"

Lysara hesitated, her eyes fixed on the fire. For a moment, Therion thought she might not answer, but then she sighed deeply.

"There's a place in the mountains," she said finally. "A sanctuary. It's hidden, protected by old magic— magic I doubt even those hellspawn can touch. If we can make it there, we'll have a chance to regroup, to plan our next move."

Therion studied her, his expression unreadable. "And what's waiting for us there? Allies? Supplies?"

Lysara shook her head. "I can't say for certain. But it's our only chance."

Therion exhaled sharply, running a hand through his hair. The weight of their predicament pressed heavily on his shoulders, but he knew Lysara was right. The capital was no longer an option. Whatever awaited them beyond the mountains, it was their best hope.

The fire crackled softly, casting dancing shadows on the cavern walls. The soldiers murmured quietly among themselves, their voices a low hum. For now, they had a moment of respite, but Therion knew it wouldn't last.

Lysara stood, her gaze distant as she stared toward the cavern's entrance. "Get some rest," she said softly. "We'll need to move at first light."

Therion nodded, though he doubted he'd find any sleep. The betrayal at the capital, the hellspawns, and the treacherous journey ahead— it all weighed heavily on his mind. But as he looked at the men gathered around the fire, battered and bruised but still alive, he knew they couldn't afford to give up.

They had survived this long. Surely that meant their Goddess had not forsaken them, hopefully that faith would be enough to see them all through this mountain.

***

A day's ride from Dowry…

A Desperate Flight

Rubelle had managed to avoid the checkpoints and the knights pursuing her by navigating the dense, overgrown forest paths. Each step deeper into the wilderness was grueling, but her daughter's well-being weighed heavier on her than the fatigue of the journey. Dalia, her bubbly ten-year-old, had grown unusually reserved over the last few days. At first, Rubelle had feared the girl might resent her for tearing her from the only life she'd known, forcing her on this perilous escape with little warning. But Dalia had surprised her.

The child was sharp beyond her years, adapting to the situation with a maturity that baffled Rubelle. Dalia didn't complain or falter. Instead, she became a pillar of calm in their storm of uncertainty, her presence grounding Rubelle in moments when fear and exhaustion threatened to overwhelm her. It was thanks to Dalia's resilience that they'd made such good time and now approached the border.

Rubelle's plan relied on the unorthodox. She wasn't heading for a checkpoint, nor did she concern herself with walls or guards. Instead, her destination was the Fairy Woods—a territory feared by most for its treacherous wards and the savage Mythenians who roamed its depths. To Rubelle, it was the closest border of man and a haven of sorts. The forest was shrouded in mystery and peril, yes, but it was also a place where she had allies. Her past missions as the Court Mage had brought her into contact with figures in the woods—beings who might offer her and Dalia shelter.

As the dense trees began to thin, revealing the faint glimmers of warding runes that marked the boundary of the Fairy Woods, Rubelle allowed herself a moment of relief. She halted her horse, glancing back at Dalia. "We're almost there," she reassured, offering a smile that she hoped masked her lingering unease. "We'll be safe soon."

But before Dalia could respond, the twang of a bowstring cut through the quiet. An arrow zipped past, so close that it tugged at the edge of Rubelle's cloak. She startled, her instincts flaring as magic surged through her veins, ready to strike.

"Don't!" a voice rang out sharply. "Think of your daughter."

Rubelle froze, her heart pounding as several knights emerged from the shadows of the trees. They moved deliberately, their weapons drawn but not raised. The man who had spoken stepped forward, his armor gleaming in the fading light.

"We suspected you'd come here," he said, his tone measured. "The border's been under watch for days. We tightened security the moment you fled. After all, you are the former Court Mage. We couldn't underestimate you."

Rubelle's mind raced as she dismounted, her movements slow and deliberate. She glanced at

Dalia, who clutched the saddle nervously, her wide eyes filled with fear. Rubelle placed a calming hand on her daughter's arm before turning to the knights, raising her hands as commanded.

"You're defenders of the realm," she said, her voice steady despite the knot forming in her stomach. "You swore an oath to protect the kingdom, its people, and its monarchs. Tell me— how can you stand by as the rightful rulers are usurped? How can you be part of this treachery?"

Her words hung in the air, and for a moment, she saw doubt flicker across their faces. The knights shifted uneasily, exchanging glances.

Finally, the lead knight spoke, his expression grim. "We share your conviction," he admitted. "But the authority cast over us leaves no room for rebellion. The power we serve binds us, just as you once served it."

Rubelle's heart sank. She had hoped to sway them, to appeal to their sense of duty. But it was clear now that they were as much prisoners of this corruption as she was its fugitive.

"I see," she murmured, her voice tinged with disappointment. A knight approached cautiously, rope in hand, to bind her. Rubelle held his gaze as she stepped forward, her expression softening into something almost regretful.

"But neither can I," she whispered.

Before the knight could react, Rubelle moved with startling speed, seizing him and twisting him into a shield. A dagger gleamed in her hand, its edge pressed against his neck.

"Release him!" one of the knights barked, their weapons rising. "You're innocent now, but you'll become a criminal if you do this!"

Rubelle ignored the warning, her grip tightening. Words of power spilled from her lips in a low chant. As the knights braced themselves, she shoved her hostage forward and unleashed a powerful gust of wind. Dust and debris exploded around her, forming a thick, blinding screen.

"Run!" she shouted, smacking her horse to spur it forward.

Dalia screamed, her voice cutting through the chaos. "Mama!"

"I'm right behind you!" Rubelle called back, already spinning to face the knights charging through the dust.

One emerged from the smoke, his sword slashing toward her. Despite her slender frame, Rubelle moved with practiced efficiency. She sidestepped the blow, catching his arm and using his armor's weight against him. With a sharp twist, she slammed him to the ground, the impact echoing through the trees.

Another knight came at her, his blade cutting dangerously close. She dodged, her magic flaring as she flung him backward with a blast of force. The air around her buzzed with energy, her spell work precise and unyielding.

The knights regrouped, their shouts growing louder as the dust began to settle. Rubelle raised her hands, her magic weaving a new incantation. This time, the wind surged in a violent wave, clearing the smoke and hurling the knights off their feet.

She didn't wait to see the aftermath. Channeling her wind magic beneath her, Rubelle leaped into the air, hovering above the forest floor. Trees blurred past as she propelled herself forward, her eyes locked on the faint silhouette of her daughter ahead.

Rubelle's determination burned brightly as she raced toward Dalia and their horse.

"After her!" She heard them jeer. "Don't let her get away!"

The shouts of the knights echoed through the dense woods, as they gave chase. Her breath came in sharp bursts, her legs trembling with exhaustion. Mimicking flight, even for a short time, was a high-level spell that drained her reserves of *mythen*. Every second took a heavier toll, but she gritted her teeth and pressed on. She couldn't falter now— not when Dalia was waiting.

Through the trees ahead, Rubelle caught a glimpse of her daughter clinging to their horse. Dalia's wide eyes brightened at the sight of her. "Mother!" she cried, her voice trembling with both relief and fear.

The girl was struggling with the reins, her small hands barely maintaining control of the skittish animal. The horse reared slightly, startled by Rubelle's sudden appearance as the spell finally gave out. Rubelle hit the ground roughly but rolled to her feet without hesitation.

"Dalia, hold on!" she yelled, her voice sharp as she rushed forward. Ignoring the searing fatigue in her limbs, she seized the reins with one hand and hoisted herself onto the saddle in a fluid motion. Pulling her daughter close, she spurred the horse forward with a sharp flick of the reins.

"Hang on tight!" Rubelle commanded.

The pounding hooves of the horse drowned out all other sounds as they tore through the forest. The knights were relentless in their pursuit, their shouts growing louder as they gained ground. Rubelle's mind raced for a solution. She couldn't outrun them forever. She needed a plan—and quickly.

Ahead, she spotted a natural dam formed by fallen logs and debris, precariously holding back a significant body of water. The sight sparked an idea, desperate and dangerous. If she could destroy the dam, it would unleash a torrent strong enough to block the knights' path— or sweep them away entirely. Though she hoped it wouldn't be the latter.

"Just a little further," she murmured to herself, guiding the horse toward the riverbank.

As they neared the dam, Rubelle began channeling a new spell. She felt the familiar hum of mythen coursing through her veins, a fierce energy gathering in her hands. The spell was ready, but as she raised her arm to release it, a sharp cry from Dalia pierced the air.

"Mother, look out!"

The warning came too late. An arrow whizzed through the air, striking Rubelle's side with brutal force. Pain exploded in her body as the arrowhead lodged deep, her spell faltering for an instant before she forced it through sheer will.

"Stay close!" she gasped, pulling Dalia into a protective embrace as the horse reared in panic. Rubelle released the spell, and with a deafening crack, the dam gave way.

The unleashed water roared like a beast, a massive wave surging forward and engulfing everything in its path. But the pain had made Rubelle's plan veer off course as the force knocked the horse off balance, sending her and Dalia tumbling into the torrent.

The icy water hit Rubelle like a hammer, stealing the breath from her lungs. She clung tightly to her daughter, her arms wrapped protectively around the girl as they were swept downstream. The river was wild and unrelenting, dragging them beneath the surface before spitting them out again further down allow with the current.

On the riverbank, the knights skidded to a halt, their expressions a mix of frustration and dismay. The leader dismounted, his gaze fixed on the chaotic waters.

"We'll track where the river ends!" one of the knights suggested, his voice sharp with urgency.

"No," the leader interjected, his tone heavy. He stood silent for a moment, fists clenching at his sides before he spoke again. "They won't survive those currents. There's no point in chasing corpses."

The knights exchanged uncertain glances but ultimately nodded in agreement. One by one, they turned away, preparing to retreat.

As the others mounted their horses, the leader lingered at the edge of the river. His stern expression wavered, and for a fleeting moment, something softer flickered in his eyes.

"Good luck," he muttered under his breath, his words barely audible over the roar of the river.

With a final, reluctant glance at the churning waters, he turned and followed his men back toward the forest, leaving the river to its secrets.

***

The Storm wouldn't let up, but in a way that was a good thing.

Though the surviving knights couldn't set out at dawn as planned, the storm gave them more time to actually rest their weary ones. These past few days had been one hell after another, but at least in this cave there was calm. The fire crackled faintly, casting flickering shadows on the cavern walls. Though the flames brought warmth, it was faint and fleeting against the chill that pressed in from the storm outside. The men sat in a loose circle, huddled close to one another, their faces marked with exhaustion and the faintest glimmers of hope. The last of their supplies were laid out on a tattered blanket—a meager spread of hardtack, dried meats, and a small flask of water.

Therion stood silently as the men divided the rations, each taking only a modest portion to ensure there was enough to go around. Despite their grim circumstances, there was no sign of complaint. These were battle-hardened soldiers, accustomed to sacrifice.

When all had been distributed, Garrish handed Therion a small piece of bread and a strip of meat. "The men left this for you," he said simply.

Therion looked at the meager offering in his hand, then at the faces of the soldiers around him. Despite the exhaustion etched into their features, there was a steadfast strength in their eyes, a resolve that refused to waver.

He rose to his feet, his voice carrying through the cavern. "Brothers," he began, "we've been through hell together. We've fought side by side, bled side by side. And now, even as the cold and hunger gnaw at us, you show me what it means to be truly unbreakable."

The men turned their eyes to him, their movements slowing as they hung onto his words.

"I am proud," Therion continued, his voice firm and steady, "proud to stand among you, proud to call you my comrades. No matter what lies ahead—whether we reach sanctuary or face death—we do so as one. Let that be the legacy we leave behind: the strength of men who refused to fall."

A hushed silence fell over the cavern, broken only by the crackling of the fire. Garrish stood then, his deep voice rumbling with a melodic cadence as he began to sing:

"Knights once bold, now march in shrouds,
To the Goddess, through storm and clouds.
Steel in hand, though hearts may rest,
they join the honored, the mighty, the blessed."

The first verse echoed softly, uncertainly, but as Garrish launched into the second, the others joined in, their voices growing in strength:

"Through fields of ash and crimson tide,
They walk as one, side by side.
Their song resounds, their spirits soar,
To join the hall of knights once more."

The chant filled the cavern, resonating off the icy walls, its rhythm steady and infectious. Therion found himself smiling despite the circumstances, the sound of their voices stirring something deep within him. For the first time in days, there was warmth in the air that had nothing to do with the fire.

He glanced to the side and noticed Lysara standing near the cave's entrance, her gaze fixed on the shimmering veil of illusion she had cast. Her face was tense, her shoulders rigid, and there was something in her eyes that gave him pause. Leaving the others to their chant, he made his way to her.

"You're not joining in?" Therion asked softly.

Without turning to him, Lysara replied, "I can feel them."

Therion's smile faded. "The hellspawn?"

She nodded, her expression darkening. "Their mythen—it's like a stench. Foul, suffocating. It's faint now, but it's growing stronger."

Therion's jaw tightened as he looked past the veil into the swirling snow beyond. "How close?"

"Not close enough to see us yet," Lysara said. She shook her head, her voice dropping. "I'm sorry for being so grim. It's just..." She hesitated, glancing at him before continuing. "I don't know how you do it, Therion. How you rally them like that. I could never inspire them the way you do."

He frowned, a faint blush coloring his cheeks. "You give me too much credit. I might be able to speak to them, but I don't have your wisdom. If it weren't for you, I'd have gotten myself killed back at the camp. In a fit of rage, no less."

Lysara tilted her head, studying him with an almost motherly patience. "You're too hard on yourself. It takes more than strength to lead men—

it takes heart. And you have that in abundance, Therion. That's why they follow you."

Therion's expression softened, but there was a flicker of doubt in his eyes. "Sometimes I think about what my wife would say if she saw me now. I can't help but feel... disappointed in myself."

Lysara reached out, resting a hand on his shoulder. "You're a fine commander," she said firmly. "And we'll get through this. Together."

Therion looked at her, the weight of her words slowly sinking in. "Where are you taking us, Lysara? Really."

Her gaze flickered back to the veil, her lips pressing into a thin line. "I don't think the capital is what we left it. But I have a friend who might be able to help us. Someone I trust."

"In the mountains?" Therion asked skeptically.

Lysara gave a wry laugh. "No, but the mountains are our best shot at getting his attention. Just believe in me, Therion. I'll get you back to your family."

Therion smiled sincerely, the tension in his shoulders easing. "Thank you, Lysara."

She gave his shoulder a reassuring squeeze before turning toward the fire. "Did I ever tell you about the time I slew a kraken in the Northern Waves?" she called out, her voice carrying through the cavern.

The men, still caught up in their chant, paused to glance her way. Garrish grinned. "Never," someone responded as a member of her army scoffed.

"With all due respect Commander. I think you're embellishing!"

"Not a chance," Lysara replied, slipping seamlessly into their banter. The soldiers laughed, their spirits lifting as they urged her to recount the story again.

Therion watched them, his heart feeling lighter than it had in days. He didn't know if this would be their last moment of peace, but for now, it was enough. The storm that had raged around them for hours finally subsided, leaving the mountain path eerily quiet and blanketed in pristine snow.

Lysara stood, brushing the frost from her armor. "We need to move. The storm bought us time, but they'll be coming."

The survivors mounted their steeds, grateful for the break in the weather. The path ahead, though treacherous, was no longer obscured by the relentless blizzard. Their pace quickened, hooves crunching over hardened snow as they pressed onward, winding higher into the mountain's unforgiving embrace.

It wasn't long before their destination came into view.

"Whoa, easy, boy…" Therion reined in his steed, his eyes widening as a colossal structure emerged from the mist. Ahead of them loomed a monumental bridge, a skeletal remnant of a forgotten age. It stretched across a chasm so deep that the bottom was lost to shadows. The bridge's ancient stonework was a masterpiece of craftsmanship, even in ruin.

Enormous pillars jutted from the abyss like sentinels of old, some cracked and tilted precariously. Arches that once bore the weight of countless travelers hung in disrepair, frost encrusting their surfaces. The entire structure seemed suspended between two towering peaks, defying the laws of nature. The wind howled through the gaps, carrying with it an almost mournful whisper, as though the bridge itself lamented its decline.

The survivors gathered at the edge of the structure, their breath visible in the frigid air. Therion dismounted, his boots crunching against the frozen ground as he approached the intricate carvings that adorned the crumbling stone.

"It's magnificent…" one of the men muttered, awe-stricken.

"It's a death trap," another countered, pointing out the gaping holes that made the bridge impassable.

Therion turned to Lysara, who was already inspecting one of the ancient columns. She knelt, brushing away layers of frost and snow to reveal faintly glowing runes etched into the surface.

"Commander Lysara," he called, his voice tinged with urgency. "What is this place?"

Lysara didn't look up, her gloved fingers tracing the runes with the precision of a scholar. "This is what the mythenians left behind," she said absently. "When the giants refused to finish their work."

"Giants?" one of the knights asked, stepping closer.

She nodded, brushing off more snow to reveal additional runes. "Legend has it the giants were commissioned to build this bridge, but their pride got the better of them. They abandoned the project, leaving it incomplete. What they didn't realize…" She trailed off, her eyes narrowing as if recalling a lesson learned long ago. Lysara finally stood, the faint glow of the runes reflecting in her determined gaze. "The mythenians wove their mythen into the foundation. Even in its ruined state, the bridge can be made whole. For a time."

The survivors exchanged uneasy glances. While Therion quietly watched the Commander work. "With the right incantation of course," Lysara added.

"And you know it?" He finally spoke.

"Why else would I bring us here?" she replied with a faint smirk, though her tone faltered. "But I fear the spell would greatly drain me."

The men murmured among themselves knowing that would mean they'd have to face the cold without her mythen keeping them warm, but Therion ignored them. He stepped closer, his voice steady.

"We don't have a choice. Do it."

Lysara nodded and moved to the center of the ruins, planting her hands firmly on the frosted ground. The others mounted their horses, ready to cross at a moment's notice. Therion stayed on foot, holding the reins of her steed in case she needed them.

Closing her eyes, Lysara began to chant. Her voice carried a melody both ancient and powerful, resonating with the runes around her. The air shimmered as unseen energy pulsed outward. The runes on the bridge responded, their faint glow intensifying with every syllable of her incantation.

A deep hum filled the air, and the ground beneath them trembled. Frost crawled across the shattered spans of the bridge, and shards of ice and stone spiraled upward from the abyss. Piece by piece, the gaps in the bridge began to knit together, forming a gleaming pathway.

The knights watched in awe as the ruins transformed before their eyes. No longer a crumbling relic, the bridge now stood as a monument to the Era of Mythen— a structure so magnificent it seemed to defy the very concept of time.

Therion's breath caught in his throat. "Incredible…"

Lysara struggled to her feet, her knees trembling from the immense strain of the spell, but she held herself upright with an air of confidence that belied her exhaustion. Mounting her horse with a sharp exhale, she looked to her men and said sternly, "We have ten minutes. No more. Move!"

There was no time to admire the breathtaking view of the ancient, restored bridge or the surrounding peaks bathed in a fleeting glow of dawn. With urgency driving their every motion, the group spurred their horses into a gallop, the rhythmic pounding of hooves echoing across the enchanted structure.

Therion rode at the front beside Lysara, his eyes darting to the rear where Garrish and a handful of knights kept watch. Despite the peril, he felt a fleeting hope. They could make it.

That hope was shattered by a guttural, bone-chilling hiss that reverberated through the chasm.

Therion's blood ran cold as his gaze shot upward. A hulking figure, hunched on all fours, scrambled along the bridge's icy pillars like a monstrous lizard. Its elongated limbs ended in wicked claws, and its eyes burned with an unholy light. A hellspawn.

"Hellspawn!" Therion bellowed, his voice carrying over the howling wind. The men reacted immediately, drawing their weapons even though they knew they were powerless against the creature without Lysara's enchantments. Their steel alone would not pierce its enchanted hide.

"Ride faster!" Therion shouted as he matched Lysara's pace, his tone sharp with urgency. "It's after you."

Lysara shot a glance upward, her expression steely as she whipped her reins and urged her horse forward. The hellspawn's predatory gaze was locked on her, its hiss growing louder as it closed the distance, ignoring the knights entirely.

Despite their efforts, the creature moved with terrifying speed. It lunged from the pillar, claws outstretched, narrowly missing Lysara as she swerved her mount. The knights scattered, but the hellspawn's scythe-like tail lashed out, slashing into the leg of Lysara's horse. The animal cried out, stumbling violently before collapsing. Lysara leapt clear with remarkable agility, rolling to her feet as the rest of the group raced ahead.

"No!" Therion shouted, pulling his horse to a halt. "If she dies, so do our chances of survival!"

The men didn't need reminding. They wheeled their mounts around, galloping back toward the commander. The hellspawn's tail whipped downward, aiming to cleave Lysara in two, but she raised her hands and summoned a barrier in time to deflect the blow. The shimmering shield flickered, betraying her weakening magic, as she scrambled to her feet and tried to put distance between herself and the creature.

Garrish twisted in his saddle, nocking an arrow and letting it fly. The missile struck the hellspawn in its flank, but it only seemed to enrage the beast. Its glowing eyes remained fixed on Lysara as it prepared to lunge again.

Therion charged in, veering his horse to the side and slashing at the creature's tail. Sparks flew as his blade glanced off the enchanted hide, eliciting a shriek of fury from the hellspawn. It reared back before swinging its tail in a wide arc, aiming to cut down as many of the knights as possible.

The deadly appendage struck Garrish's horse, sending the knight tumbling to the frozen ground. Another knight wasn't so lucky; the scythe-like tail took his head clean off, his lifeless body toppling from the saddle. Garrish rolled to his feet, wincing as he clutched his side where blood seeped through his armor.

The hellspawn's tail smashed into one of the bridge's pillars, sending cracks spider webbing through the icy structure. With a deafening groan, the pillar gave way, collapsing onto the creature and pinning it beneath tons of rubble. For a moment, silence reigned, and the group dared to hope the danger was over.

Their hopes were dashed as the hellspawn's dismembered parts began to writhe and pull together, the foul magic regenerating the beast before their eyes.

"The spell's coming undone!" Lysara shouted, her voice strained as the runes on the bridge flared erratically. The ancient magic sustaining the structure wavered, the ice and stone groaning ominously as they began to crumble back into the abyss.

"We're losing the bridge!" a knight cried, panic creeping into his voice.

Therion spurred his horse forward, pulling Lysara onto the saddle behind him. He hesitated, glancing back to ensure Garrish had remounted his injured but still-standing steed. The knight's face was pale, but his eyes burned with determination as he urged his horse onward.

The group fled, the sound of collapsing stone and the hellspawn's unearthly screeches driving them forward. Garrish's horse lagged behind, its movements hampered by its injuries, but the knight showed no sign of slowing.

"It's just ahead!" Therion roared, the far end of the bridge coming into view. Victory seemed within reach—until Garrish glanced back and saw the hellspawn fully regenerated and in pursuit.

The knight's expression hardened. "It's right behind us," he called.

"Forget it! We're almost there!" Therion shouted.

Garrish shook his head. "No, brother. You're almost there."

Before Therion could respond, Garrish pulled his horse to a stop and dismounted. Drawing his sword, he turned to face the oncoming hellspawn. "For O'Rivera!" he bellowed, his voice echoing with defiance. "For honor!"

Therion twisted in his saddle, horror flashing across his face. "Garrish, no!"

He nearly stopped, but Lysara seized the reins and spurred the horse forward, her voice firm. "He's buying us time. Don't waste it."

Therion's heart wrenched as he looked back. Garrish charged at the hellspawn, his sword gleaming in the fading light. The creature lunged, its claws slashing downward, but Garrish dodged with surprising agility. His blade struck true, carving into the beast's side and drawing another enraged screech. The hellspawn lashed out with its tail, and Garrish met it head-on, his blade sparking against the enchanted appendage.

The bridge shuddered violently, cracks racing through the ice and stone. With a deafening crack, the section beneath Garrish and the hellspawn gave way. Both plummeted into the abyss below, their forms swallowed by the shadows.

Therion and the others reached the far side of the bridge just as it collapsed entirely, leaving only a few precarious remnants clinging to the mountainside just as they'd found it. If the survivors that set out together that morning, only five had made it across the bridge.

The group dismounted, their breaths ragged from strain and cold as they turned to stare at the void where the bridge once stood. Therion's hands trembled as he gripped the reins, his mind reeling as the cold, Lysara's magic had protected them from, finally berated him too. Garrish's final words echoed in his ears, a haunting reminder of the sacrifice that had bought them their survival.

Lysara placed a hand on his shoulder, her voice quiet but resolute. "We have to keep moving. Garrish didn't give his life for us to falter now."

Therion nodded, swallowing the lump in his throat. "For O'Rivera," he murmured, echoing the fallen knight's battle cry. The others repeated the phrase, their voices tinged with sorrow and determination.

He sheathed his sword with a sharp motion, his expression hardening into a mask.

"Commander Lysara is right. We've got to keep moving," he resolved to the survivors, turning away from the ruined bridge. "I fear the others must have heard the commotion."

Lysara hesitated at the grim realization, but she too quickly accepted the sacrifices that'd been made to get them all this far. "You're right… I bet," she replied quietly, her tone heavy with unspoken grief as she rode ahead leading their group through the bitter cold in hope that they might all survive this perilous ordeal in the end.

Chapter Eight: Sanctuary

Rubelle awoke to the faint sensation of shaking. Her eyes fluttered open, the world around her blurred and muffled. The cold hit her first, sharp and biting, followed by the wet, clammy feel of her clothes clinging to her skin. She blinked a few times before her vision settled on Dalia's pale, tear-streaked face.

"Mom, wake up! Please!" Dalia cried, her small hands gripping Rubelle's shoulders.

"I'm... awake," Rubelle murmured weakly, managing a faint smile for her daughter's sake.

But the moment she tried to move, pain surged through her side, and she hissed sharply. Her hand drifted to her ribs, coming away slick with blood. The arrow wound. Memories of the icy river rushed back— the fall, the desperate pull of the current, and the frantic struggle to get Dalia to shore.

She shivered violently, her body trembling as she forced herself to sit up. "Dalia," she said, her voice hoarse, "Are you hurt?"

"No," Dalia replied, her lips trembling. "But you're bleeding. It's bad, Mom."

Rubelle glanced down at the jagged tear in her side. Blood seeped from the wound, the edges raw and inflamed. Her fingers trembled as she pressed against it, summoning what little mythen she had left. Whispering the incantation, she willed the magic to respond, but the faint glow fizzled and died. Her reserves were utterly drained.

"How long was I unconscious?" she rasped, her voice strained.

"I don't know," her daughter replied, worry etched into her young face. "You just laid back after we got out of the water."

Rubelle's gaze drifted downstream, her thoughts clouded. She remembered the drop into the freezing current and the frantic escape before that. Had they gained enough distance from their pursuers? Her head swam, but the sharp, throbbing pain in her side dragged her focus back to the present.

She pressed harder against the wound, but blood continued to seep through her fingers. It was deep, far too serious to ignore. Her mythen was spent, and healing herself was out of reach. Leaving it untreated wasn't an option.

But there was one other way.

Her breath hitched as the thought took hold. It wasn't a solution she wanted to consider, but desperation left no room for hesitation. Her fingers tightened over the wound, trembling at the prospect of what she was about to do.

Noting the worry in her daughter's eyes, Rubelle forced herself to meet her gaze. "It's going to be okay," she whispered, though her voice lacked conviction.

Steeling herself, she swallowed the lump of dread rising in her throat. Her magic couldn't heal her now, but there was another, far more painful way to survive. She braced for the agony to come.

This was going to hurt.

"Now listen Dalia," she said, her voice steady despite the pain, "I need you to look away, or- better still… close your eyes."

"What? Why?"

"Just do it, sweetheart. Don't look."

Dalia hesitated, but the urgency in her mother's tone made her comply. She squeezed her eyes shut, her hands clutching the fabric of her skirt tightly.

Rubelle grabbed a small branch that'd swept up near them, her fingers trembling as she ignited it with a weak spark of mythen. The tip glowed red-hot, and the smell of burning wood filled the air. She took a steadying breath, her grip tightening on the branch.

"Mom, what are you doing?" Dalia's voice quivered with fear.

"It's okay, Dalia. I promise I'm fine," Rubelle lied, pressing the searing branch to her wound.

A muffled scream tore from her throat as the pain exploded through her. Tears streamed down her face as she gritted her teeth, her body shaking violently. The smell of burnt flesh mingled with the charred wood, and Dalia began to sob.

"Stop it! Stop hurting yourself!" Dalia cried, reaching for her.

"I'm fine," Rubelle rasped, her voice strained but firm. "It's done."

She tossed the branch aside, her breaths shallow and uneven. The bleeding had stopped, the wound cauterized, but the pain lingered, sharp and unrelenting. She reached out to Dalia, pulling her close despite her own agony.

"See? I'm okay now," she whispered, stroking her daughter's hair.

Dalia shook her head, tears soaking into Rubelle's torn dress. "You're not okay. You're hurt. You're in pain!"

"Pain means I'm alive," Rubelle said with a faint smile, though it didn't reach her eyes. "That's what matters."

Forcing herself to her feet, she stepped forward briskly to lean heavily on a nearby tree for support. Dalia quickly noticed and held unto her mother's hand while Rubelle caught her breath. Rubelle groaned. "We need to keep moving."

As she spoke her eyes examined the forest looming around them, dark and silent save for the rustling of leaves in the wind. Rubelle was quite sure where they were, or which direction pointed in their intended direction. She felt lightheaded, her vision swimming, but she couldn't stop now.

"How long was I out?" Rubelle asked again, trying to keep her voice steady.

"I don't know," Dalia replied, her voice small.

"Guess, sweetheart. Just guess."

Dalia hesitated, frowning in concentration. "Maybe... ten minutes?"

Rubelle's stomach tightened. Ten minutes. Not enough time to have drifted far from the knights. They could already be searching the riverbanks. Her chest ached with the thought of the chase resuming. "We have to move," she said, her voice firmer now. "We can't stay here."

Dalia nodded reluctantly, falling into step beside her mother as they trudged into the woods. Rubelle pushed forward, though each step was a battle against the dizziness threatening to consume her. Her breaths came in shallow gasps, her body screaming for rest.

"Mom, are you okay?" Dalia asked, her voice tinged with panic.

Rubelle opened her mouth to respond, but the words wouldn't come. The world around her blurred and tilted as her strength began to falter. Her knees buckled, and she caught herself against a tree, clutching Dalia's hand tightly.

"I'm fine," she lied again, though she could barely hear her own voice over the pounding in her head.

The shadows of the forest seemed to grow darker, deeper, as if they were closing in around her. Her grip on Dalia tightened, and she began to mutter under her breath, her words slurred and uneven.

"Mom?" Dalia's voice was distant now, a faint echo in the void.

Rubelle clung to the last threads of her consciousness, her trembling arms pulling Dalia close as the spell spilled from her lips. The words were slurred, her strength fading fast, but a faint shimmer of light enveloped them both. The protective veil flickered like a dying flame, fragile and weak, as she unintentionally dragged Dalia down with her.

"Huh? Mom, stay with me! Please!" Dalia's voice cracked with desperation, her small hands shaking Rubelle's shoulders, but there was no response. Rubelle's body had given out entirely, and they crumpled together onto the forest floor.

Darkness seeped into Rubelle's mind, an oppressive coldness that smothered her thoughts. She drifted in a void, weightless and suffocated, her awareness flickering like the veil she had conjured. It felt endless, a realm devoid of time, until a sensation—vivid and unnatural—pulled her sharply into focus.

This was no ordinary unconsciousness.

Rubelle found herself standing, though her body felt sluggish and unfamiliar. The void around her twisted and churned, a maelstrom of shadows so alive they seemed to breathe. Her breath quickened, and she froze as dread clawed its way up her spine. She wasn't alone.

A sinister presence filled the space, suffocating in its malice. The shadows coalesced into a towering form, one she recognized all too well. It wasn't the stalking shadow from the forest but the source of it, a behemoth of pure darkness. Its glowing eyes burned like twin suns, piercing through her soul with cruel delight.

It stared at her as if savoring the moment, a hunter relishing its catch. Then, it spoke.

Found you...

The voice rumbled through the void, shaking the very essence of her being. Rubelle's knees buckled, and though she tried to scream, no sound escaped her lips. The darkness surged forward, swallowing her whole.

***

An hour's ride from the Bridge of Ruins...

"It's here..." Lysara announced, her voice carrying an odd mix of relief and urgency as she gestured ahead.

The group staggered to a halt, the weary survivors following her lead. Before them lay a monumental shrine nestled in the heart of the mountain. Towering pillars encircled the shrine, their surfaces etched with intricate runes that pulsed faintly, as though ancient *mythen* still coursed through their lines. Unlike the snowy expanse surrounding it, the shrine stood untouched by winter's grasp.

The air grew warm, like the gentle heat of a summer afternoon. The stark contrast was disorienting but undeniably pleasant. Wildflowers bloomed in vibrant clusters along the ground, their bright colors painting a surreal image against the otherwise frigid landscape. As the group stepped closer, a tangible energy washed over them, a rejuvenating force that seemed to breathe life back into their exhausted bodies.

Therion paused mid-step, his hand instinctively reaching for the wound on his head. His fingers met smooth, unbroken skin where there should have been torn flesh. Startled, he glanced at the others and saw similar expressions of confusion and awe. Cuts and bruises vanished as if swept away by the invisible power radiating from the shrine.

One of the men let out a delighted cry and darted toward a nearby berry bush, greedily plucking and eating the ripe fruit. His enthusiasm stirred the others, who quickly joined him, laughing and cheering as they indulged.

But Therion's focus remained on Lysara. She had knelt to the ground the moment they arrived, her hands methodically carving symbols into the earth. It was then he noticed the blackened blood staining the snow beneath her. His eyes widened in alarm.

"You're still bleeding!" he exclaimed, striding toward her. He grabbed her wrist, careful but firm, stealing a glance at the wound she was trying to hide. Unlike the others, her injuries weren't healing.

"The *mythen* here heals wounds," Lysara said calmly, pulling her arm free. "But it doesn't regenerate. My body's too far gone." She returned to her etching, as if her words were nothing more than a statement of fact.

Therion knelt beside her, his voice low but urgent. "What can I do to help?"

She paused, looking at him thoughtfully for a moment. "When I accepted this mission," she began, "I imagined you as young, rash, and cocky. The kind of man who'd thought about his pride and glory." A faint smile touched her lips. "But I was wrong. You've surprised me, Therion. You're a good leader... and a better man than I expected."

Her words left him momentarily speechless.

Lysara turned back to her runes, her movements precise. "The least you can do is ensure that you and the rest of our people make it out of here. Make things right."

Before Therion could respond, a bone-chilling roar tore through the mountains like a harbinger of doom. The sound reverberated through the air and seemed to settle deep in their chests, a primal reminder of their mortality. The group froze, their breaths hanging visibly in the cold air, as the sound carried an unspoken promise of violence.

Through the thick, rolling fog ahead, massive forms began to materialize. At first, they were nothing more than vague shapes, ominous and shadowed, but as they lumbered closer, the light of the shrine revealing them in all their grotesque glory.

Hellspawns.

Their twisted, sinewy bodies seemed to ripple with dark energy, their malformed limbs moving unnaturally as they advanced. At the head of the group was a creature they all recognized. The same Hellspawn that'd given chase on the bridge and they'd thought had fallen to its demise. Its presence made the air feel heavier, as though the creature's malice had a physical weight.

Therion felt a surge of anger cut through his fear, his hand tightening around the hilt of his sword until his knuckles whitened. His glare locked onto the creature with an intensity that could have melted steel. The others, sensing the change in him, instinctively fell into defensive stances, their weapons at the ready.

But then, the Hellspawns stopped.

They loomed just beyond the ancient stone pillars that surrounded the shrine, their movements halting as though an unseen force held them at bay. It wasn't hesitation or fear— Hellspawns knew neither— but something else, something that kept them tethered to the shadows beyond the sacred boundary.

One of the creatures let out a guttural hiss, its elongated jaws opening wide enough to reveal rows of jagged, blackened teeth. An ominous glow began to build within its throat, dark and pulsating like a malevolent heart. The group barely had time to brace themselves as the creature released a torrent of seething black mythen toward the shrine.

The attack surged forward, an inky wave of destruction aimed directly at them. Yet, just as it reached the edge of the shrine's perimeter, it struck an invisible barrier. There was no sound of impact, only a sudden, blinding flash of light.

The mythen recoiled violently, as if repelled by the very sanctity of the shrine. It twisted back toward its origin, transforming mid-air into a torrent of searing flames. The Hellspawn let out an ear-splitting shriek as the fire engulfed its body, a sound that clawed at their eardrums.

The creature thrashed wildly, its grotesque form writhing in agony. Snow melted into steam around it as it desperately tried to extinguish the flames, clawing at its own burning flesh. But nothing worked. The fire burned with an unearthly intensity, consuming the beast until it finally collapsed in a heap, reduced to a smoldering husk.

A tentative cheer erupted from the knights, their voices shaky but filled with relief. For a brief moment, hope sparked amidst the despair.

But the victory was short-lived.

The remaining Hellspawns moved closer, their glowing, unblinking eyes fixed on the charred remains of their fallen kin. At first, the knights thought the creatures might be mourning. They gathered around the carcass, their towering forms silent and still.

Then the first Hellspawn bent down, its jaws tearing into the blackened flesh with a sickening crunch. The others followed, their grotesque feast punctuated by the wet sounds of tearing meat and the low, guttural growls of satisfaction.

The knights' cheers died in their throats, replaced by a horrified silence. Therion's grip tightened on his sword as he forced himself to look away from the monstrous display.

"What in the—" one of the men whispered, his voice trembling with disgust.

The creatures devoured their fallen comrade with terrifying fervor, their bodies twitching and convulsing as they consumed. Pale-faced, Therion grimaced. "If they can do that to their own..." His voice trailed off, leaving the unspoken horror hanging in the air.

Lysara was still kneeling by the runes, and didn't look up. She could feel her strength waning but was determined to finish her spell before succumbing to her injuries. "The ward will only hold a short while," she said firmly, though the worried undertone was too evident. "I just I can finish this before it comes to that."

The tension in the air was palpable.

Every knight kept their eyes on the Hellspawns, watching as the creatures finished their gruesome feast. As they turned their attention back to the shrine, the effect of their meal became horrifyingly clear. Their bodies swelled grotesquely, muscles bulging and bones cracking as they transformed. The runes etched into their skin glowed a menacing red, and their claws extended into razor-sharp blades.

"They're evolving," one knight muttered, his voice barely audible over the pounding of his own heartbeat. Therion tightened his grip on his sword, his jaw set. "Be ready," he ordered, his voice steady despite the fear clawing at his chest.

The Hellspawns advanced again, their monstrous forms testing the barrier. Sparks flew as they pressed against the invisible wall, snarling in frustration as the ward held firm. But with each attempt, the energy around the shrine flickered slightly, the runes etched into the pillars dimming for a fraction of a second.

"Lysara," Therion called, his voice strained. "How much longer?"

She didn't answer immediately, her focus entirely on the runes she was carving. Finally, she looked up, her expression grim. "Just hold them off if the ward fails, this is our only hope—" She coughed, blackened blood staining her lips.

She was dying, but it was just as she said. Whatever spell she was working on was their last hope of survival. The knights exchanged uneasy glances. The flickering grew more pronounced, the Hellspawns' relentless attacks taking their toll. The question hung heavily over them all— would the wards hold? —or would they have to fight for their lives once more?

***

Back at the Castle...

Oriana lingered on her balcony, the tips of her fingers pressed against her lips as she chewed her nails— a habit unbecoming of a princess, yet one she couldn't break when her stress got too high. Her eyes darted down to the streets in the distance, where life carried on as if nothing had changed. She imagined the Merchants called out their wares, and children darted through the crowds in laughter. All blissfully unaware of the fact that their entire realm tilted on the verge of destruction.

Unaware that their monarchs were dead.

Unaware of how suddenly this peace could be snuffed away.

"Dear O'Rivera." Oriana prayed, her stomach churned at the thought. She was still shaken by it all, in fact she was still struggled to accept any of it. But wishful thinking could never undo the fact that her parents were cut down in a vile act of treason. Yet, their bodies had not been mourned, their deaths not announced. The throne had been stolen in the dead of night by her brother. And yet, the people below carried on as though the world hadn't shifted beneath their feet.

"Give me strength Goddess." She wrapped her arms around herself, trying to banish the memory of her vision— the terrible, vivid nightmare that had gripped her just days before. At the time, she thought waking from it had been the most scared she'd ever be. But now, confined to her chambers like a prisoner, she realized there were far more terrifying things than the thought of oblivion.

Her thoughts lingered on Rubelle.

The girl was in danger. Oriana could feel it in her very bones, the weight of Rubelle's suffering pressing against her chest. The shadow had made it abundantly clear that it'd overheard their conversation, and Oriana knew it was only a matter of time before Charon discovered the truth of her plans now.

The sound of the door opening pulled her sharply from her thoughts. She turned, her glare already forming as her brother entered the room uninvited.

Charon was as commanding as ever, his sharp features and dark hair slicked back with precision. His pale blue eyes swept the room before landing on her untouched meal, still sitting on the table where the servants had left it. His jaw clenched, and his glower deepened.

"You haven't eaten in days," he said, his voice tight with irritation.

"Why does it matter to you?" Oriana snapped, her tone laced with venom. "Do you plan to fatten me up before sacrificing me to your so-called god?"

Charon's eyes flashed with anger, but his voice cracked when he snapped back, "I would never."

"Never." Oriana's laugh was humorless. "I never would have expected you to do *any* of this. Yet here we are."

The words hung heavy in the air, a tense silence settling between them. Charon's face darkened, but then his gaze dropped to her hand, which was wrapped tightly in bandages.

"How are your fingers healing?" he asked, his voice softer but still guarded.

Oriana raised her injured hand but didn't respond, holding it up for him to see before letting it drop. Charon scowled and moved toward the table, reaching for the tray of food. The meal, once an impressive display of culinary skill, was now on the verge of spoiling. A bowl of creamy soup had congealed, and the roast meat looked dull and unappetizing. He plucked a few grapes from the bunch, popping one into his mouth as he regarded her.

"You're angry," he said after a moment. "That's understandable."

"Understandable?" Oriana hissed, taking a step closer to him. "I'm being *held hostage* in my own room!"

Charon set the grapes down and straightened, his expression hardening. "You have the freedom to roam the castle, just as you did before I took the throne."

"Freedom? Charon you call this freedom?" Oriana's voice rose, her eyes narrowing. "With your knights breathing down my neck everywhere I go? That's no freedom at all."

Charon's patience snapped. "You're ungrateful!" he bellowed. "Everything I'm doing—*everything*— is for you! For Orivera!"

Oriana stepped closer, her expression fierce. "Don't you dare play patriot with me," she said, her voice cold and cutting. "This has *nothing* to do with Orivera. This is all for you and your thirst for power."

Charon's hand slammed into the edge of the tray, sending it crashing to the floor. The remnants of the meal scattered, the sound echoing through the room.

"The veil is weakening!" he shouted, his voice raw. "Even without my interference, it is bound to break!"

Oriana stared at him, shocked by the sudden outburst.

"I saw it," Charon continued, his voice trembling. "The kingdom in flames. Man and mythen crushed beneath the Fallen's feet like we were nothing. Insignificant."

His shoulders heaved as he struggled to compose himself. For a brief moment, Oriana saw something she hadn't seen in her brother in a long time— fear.

"You've seen it too," he said, his voice quieter now.

Oriana's breath hitched. Her brother was telling the truth— by some cruel fate he'd also seen her vision, the same nightmare that had haunted her waking hours. Charon quickly wiped at his eyes, straightening his posture as though erasing any trace of vulnerability. "I struck a deal," he said firmly. "For all our sakes."

Oriana's heart sank. "What deal?"

Charon turned away from her, his expression unreadable. "It doesn't matter."

"Yes, it does!" she insisted, her voice rising with desperation. "Charon, please I need you to understand that it's playing you. It doesn't care—"

"I actually came to tell you something," he interrupted, his tone brisk. "The key you sought to hide might be closer than you think. A knight from the wall claims he has word on Rubelle, so I'm off to receive the good news."

Oriana froze, her pulse quickening. "Rubelle?" Charon didn't wait for her to respond. He moved toward the door, his hand resting on the handle. "Charon, wait!" Oriana called after him, her voice breaking. "Please do not hurt her!"

But he didn't turn around.

"Goodnight, sister," he said coldly before shutting the door behind him.

The sound of the lock clicking into place was like a dagger to her heart. Oriana threw herself at the door, slamming her fist into it as she yelled for him to come ack. This was his way of punishing her, making her worry. And she hated him for how effective it was. Trapped inside there was no way for her to know if he even spoke the truth. She sank down in front of the door as a myriad of thoughts went through her head.

The vision she had seen was a nightmare too vile for anyone to bear. She had vowed to prevent it, to fight with every fiber of her being to keep it from becoming reality. But now she realized that same vision had driven her brother into the Fallen Son's hands. She worried for her friend.

And she couldn't help but wonder if her brother was truly too far gone to be saved.

***

The night was cold and heavy with an eerie stillness. Shadows stretched long across the forest floor, and the occasional rustle of leaves whispered secrets to the wind. Yet, for Rubelle, none of this existed. In her restless unconsciousness, she floated in a place free of worry. She felt no chill, no fear. Her mind, untethered from the physical world, replayed fragments of memories—some hazy, others sharp. For a brief, precious moment, nothing mattered beyond these fleeting images.

When awareness began to seep back into her, it did so gently at first. Rubelle stirred, her body weighted with exhaustion but unburdened by the sharp, searing pain she had last felt. She groaned softly and blinked, her vision blurry as the flickering glow of firelight pulled her into the present. A small fire crackled nearby, its flames dancing in mesmerizing, fluid patterns. The light wasn't the usual orange-yellow of natural fire—it shimmered with a bluish hue, ethereal and almost alive.

Rubelle pushed herself up onto one elbow, her movements sluggish. The air felt different here, warm despite the surrounding chill. Her gaze dropped to her side, and she froze. Where a grievous wound had once been, there was now only smooth skin. A faint pink scar marked the spot, its presence the only evidence of what she had endured. A sharp gasp escaped her lips, and her fingers trembled as they traced the scar. Her heart raced as she tried to make sense of the impossible.

Her eyes flicked back to the fire. It burned steadily, the wood beneath it untouched. Her breath hitched as realization struck her.

"Mythen," she murmured, her voice hoarse. Fires imbued with mythen were rare, requiring great skill to conjure and sustain. Rubelle's mind reeled. She certainly hadn't conjured it—she had barely been alive. Her last memory was of collapsing near the riverbank, succumbing to her injuries as her strength gave out. Yet here she was, healed and somewhere entirely different. She strained her ears but heard no rushing water. Whoever had brought her here had moved her far from where she had fallen.

Her chest tightened. "Dalia?" she called, her voice breaking with urgency. Panic laced her words as she sat upright, searching the shadows. "Dalia!"

"Mummy!" The voice was small but clear, and Rubelle's heart swelled with relief. A rustling sound came from the edge of the clearing, and moments later, a figure emerged. It was Dalia, her tiny arms wrapped around a berry bush she struggled to carry.

"You're awake!" Dalia cried, abandoning the bush in her excitement. She darted forward, throwing herself into Rubelle's arms.

Rubelle clutched her daughter tightly, tears welling in her eyes. "My sweetheart," she whispered, her voice trembling as she held Dalia close. Relief coursed through her, overwhelming and pure. She pulled back just enough to look her daughter over, checking for injuries. Finding none, she hugged Dalia again, as if afraid to let her go.

For a moment, the world felt whole again. The terror and confusion receded, leaving only the warmth of their embrace. But as the minutes passed, questions began to surface, clawing their way to the forefront of Rubelle's mind.

She gently cupped Dalia's face, her thumbs brushing against her cheeks. "Where are we? And how did you start that fire?"

Dalia tilted her head, her expression puzzled. "I didn't start it," she said simply. "Root did."

Rubelle's brow furrowed. "Root?" she echoed. The name was unfamiliar, and she looked around the clearing, suddenly alert.

As if summoned by the mention of his name, a deep, groaning sound resonated from the shadows. Rubelle's head whipped around, her breath catching as a massive figure stepped into the light. A towering Treant emerged, his bark-like skin glistening faintly in the bluish glow of the fire. His gnarled arms cradled an assortment of fruits, and his glowing amber eyes radiated an ancient wisdom. Each step he took made the ground tremble faintly, his presence both awe-inspiring and humbling.

Rubelle stared, speechless. She had heard stories of Treants— ancient guardians of the forest— but had never imagined meeting one. They were reclusive creatures, their existence almost mythical to most.

The Treant groaned softly, his voice a deep rumble that echoed like the creak of ancient wood. The sound seemed to resonate through the clearing, commanding attention.

Dalia stepped forward, her face lighting up with understanding. "He's asking if your wound healed properly," she explained, turning to Rubelle with a bright smile.

Rubelle's mouth opened and closed several times before she found her voice. "It... it did," she stammered, her hand instinctively brushing over her side. "Thank you, Root."

Dalia looked back at the Treant, speaking to him in a fluid, melodic tone that made Rubelle's heart skip a beat. It was Mythenian, the ancient language of the forest—one she had never taught her daughter.

"Dalia," Rubelle said slowly, her eyes narrowing in confusion. "You speak Mythenian?"

Her daughter turned to her, puzzled. "No," she said matter-of-factly. "Why do you ask?"

Rubelle hesitated. "You... you were just speaking it."

Dalia frowned, as if trying to remember. "I was just thanking him for you," she said innocently, as if it were the simplest thing in the world.

Before Rubelle could press further, the Treant groaned again, bowing his massive head. He lowered the fruits he carried onto the ground—a generous offering of wild berries, figs, and fruits Rubelle couldn't identify.

"Thank you," Rubelle said softly, her voice filled with gratitude as she reached for a fig. Its surface was smooth and glistening with dew, and as she bit into it, a burst of sweetness filled her mouth. The taste was vivid, almost overwhelming in its richness. She hadn't realized how hungry she was until that moment.

The Treant watched her quietly, his amber eyes unreadable. Dalia sat beside her mother, happily picking at a cluster of berries.

While they ate, Dalia explained what had happened after Rubelle lost consciousness.

"When you fainted, I didn't know what to do. I was so scared, but I wouldn't leave your side. I prayed to the Goddess and cried for help. And then, out of nowhere, Root heard me!"

Her voice was animated, her hands gesturing excitedly as she recounted the events. "I told him we were heading for the border, and he said he'd help. He treated your wound and then carried us most of the way here."

Rubelle blinked, her mind struggling to keep up with the flood of information. "He carried us?" she asked, her voice a mixture of disbelief and awe.

Dalia nodded enthusiastically, her eyes sparkling.

Rubelle turned her gaze back to the Treant, who was now sitting cross-legged a short distance away. His massive form was partially silhouetted by the firelight, and his bark-like skin glowed faintly in the flickering flames. Root's calm, protective presence seemed to extend beyond their small clearing, keeping whatever monsters might lurk in the shadows at bay.

"He saved us," Rubelle whispered, her voice trembling with gratitude. She could hardly believe the turn of events.

"I… I don't know how to thank you," she said, her voice breaking with sincerity as she addressed the towering figure.

The Treant let out a deep, resonant groan that seemed to echo through the trees. Dalia quickly translated; her tone cheerful. "He says you don't need to thank him. He was happy to help."

Rubelle felt a lump form in her throat. She hadn't felt this kind of luck in so long—it was like a gift from the Goddess herself. She silently offered a prayer. *Thank you, O'Rivera,* she thought, her heart swelling with gratitude.

Steeling herself, Rubelle pressed her hands against the ground, bracing to stand. The motion caught Dalia's attention, and the Treant let out a low, cautioning growl.

Dalia spun around, her hands on her hips. "Mama, what are you doing?" she snapped. "Root's right—you're too tired to move!"

Rubelle sighed and sank back down with a wince. "I'm fine, Dalia. I just—"

"No, you're not!" Dalia interrupted, crossing her arms and fixing her mother with a stern glare. "You need to rest."

Rubelle blinked in surprise. She had only ever seen her daughter this adamant when she wanted a treat back home. The forcefulness in her voice gave Rubelle pause, and a quick glance at Root confirmed that the Treant agreed with the little girl. His glowing amber eyes seemed to soften as he emitted another low groan.

"Alright," Rubelle relented, leaning back against the tree behind her. "I'll rest. But only because you're both ganging up on me."

Dalia beamed, her triumphant smile lighting up the clearing.

Rubelle reached out and pulled her daughter into a gentle hug. "Thank you, sweet girl," she whispered, her voice heavy with emotion. Relief and gratitude flowed through her as she held Dalia close. For a moment, all the fear and uncertainty melted away.

After a moment, Dalia wriggled free of her mother's embrace and darted over to Root, who had risen to his full, towering height. He motioned with one of his gnarled, branch-like arms, pointing into the distance beyond the clearing.

Dalia gasped, her excitement palpable. "Mama! It's so close!"

Rubelle frowned, her brow furrowing. "What's close?"

Dalia turned to her, practically bouncing with enthusiasm. "The border! Root says it's just over that hill!"

Rubelle followed her daughter's gaze, her eyes landing on the silhouette of a rocky ridge bathed in pale moonlight. She exhaled slowly, the sight filling her with a sense of relief so profound it nearly brought tears to her eyes.

"You're right," she said softly. "We're that close."

Dalia nodded, her joy shining like a beacon. "We're almost there, Mama. We're going to make it!"

Rubelle leaned back against the tree, her body finally allowing itself to relax. For the first time in what felt like days, she let out a small, tired laugh. "Thank the Goddess," she murmured. Her eyes drifted shut, and a faint smile played on her lips.

As exhaustion tugged at her once more, a small nagging sensation pricked at the edge of her mind. It felt like there was something important she was overlooking, something just out of reach. But the thought was fleeting, overshadowed by the overwhelming sense of gratitude and relief she felt in the moment.

She glanced at Dalia, who was now chatting happily with Root, her tiny hands gesturing animatedly as she told him something that made his glowing eyes flicker warmly. Rubelle allowed herself to hope, for the first time in a long time. They were safe, and the border was within reach. Soon, they would be out of danger, free to rest and rebuild their lives.

Certain that everything would be over soon, Rubelle let the steady crackle of the fire and the gentle murmur of her daughter's voice lull her into a sense of peace.

Chapter Nine: Demons at the Border.

The rest of the way to the border was a lot quieter than Rubelle expected.

With their newfound companion, the mother and daughter duo found their trek through the forest unexpectedly smooth, as though the oppressive wilds had bent to accommodate them. Root, for all his gentle demeanor, was an awe-inspiring presence. His towering form and the creak of his limbs exuded a quiet power that seemed to demand respect, a power that kept even the boldest of the forest's predators at bay. Rubelle marveled at how the Treant, despite his size, moved with surprising grace, shaping their path with the dexterity of his vines and the subtle influence of his mythen.

Traversing difficult terrain became effortless. When they encountered sharp inclines or uneven ground, Root would simply lift them, cradling them in the safety of his mossy embrace. Rubelle couldn't help but feel a pang of envy—how effortlessly he seemed to command the natural world, molding it with care and precision. Watching him interact with the forest left her spellbound, like a pupil observing a master at work. Had it not been for her urgent quest, she might have begged to stay, to learn from this majestic being who carried an aura of ancient wisdom.

Birdsong punctuated the quiet as they moved, and the occasional rustling hinted at hidden creatures darting about the undergrowth. For the first time in what felt like an eternity, Dalia was at ease, her laughter bubbling up as Root entertained her with playful gestures. He extended a vine for her to balance on, forming loops and spirals as she giggled with delight. Even his smallest movements seemed imbued with a thoughtful grace that captivated the child.

Rubelle, however, could not share in her daughter's unburdened joy. Though the surroundings were serene, an unshakable unease churned in her chest. She couldn't quite place the source of it—until fragments of her recent encounter began creeping back into focus.

The memory struck like a cold wind: the inky void that had swallowed her during her collapse. Not a dream, she realized with dawning dread, but something far more sinister. Her nightmare was an encounter, a brush with some dark, unrelenting force. For days, it had hidden from her conscious mind, lurking like a parasite in the corners of her thoughts. Now, as they neared the border, its presence stirred. She couldn't discern if it was her returning strength or Root's healing magic that had loosened its grip, but the closer they came to their destination, the more the shadow clawed at her resolve.

"Are you okay, Mummy?"

Dalia's voice jolted Rubelle from her spiraling thoughts. The little girl peered down from atop Root's head, her wide eyes filled with concern.

Rubelle forced a smile, masking the storm within her. "Just a headache," she replied quickly, brushing off the question.

Dalia tilted her head, unconvinced. "Are you sure? You look… worried."

"I'm fine," Rubelle insisted, her voice firm yet hollow. She avoided her daughter's gaze, turning her focus instead to the forest ahead.

Even as she spoke, the uneasy rhythm of her heart betrayed her. She was not fine— not even close. And Dalia wasn't easily fooled. Rubelle could feel her daughter's watchful eyes lingering on the back of her head.

Root grumbled something low and resonant, the vibrations carrying an unspoken meaning. Dalia, perched atop the treant's broad shoulders, cocked her head and insisted he put her down.

"Root says he wants to help," she announced as she hopped to the ground, her tone as matter-of-fact as though discussing the weather.

Rubelle hesitated, her gaze fixed on the treant's amber eyes, their faint glow radiating warmth and sincerity. "How so?" she asked, her voice cautious yet curious.

Root didn't reply directly. His body shifted slightly, a rustling of leaves and creaking of wood betraying his uncertainty. For all his wisdom, the treant seemed unsure how to ease Rubelle's obvious distress. Yet as his presence lingered, a memory surged to the forefront of Rubelle's mind—vivid, clear, and oddly comforting.

"Dalia," Rubelle said thoughtfully, the contemplative edge in her voice catching her daughter's attention.

"Yes, Mama?"

"Can you ask Root something for me?"

Dalia tilted her head. "What do you want me to ask him?"

Rubelle hesitated, weighing her words carefully before continuing. "Ask him if it's true that treant sap can act as a powerful mythen booster."

Dalia, her brow furrowing slightly in confusion, nodded obediently and turned to Root. She relayed the question in her usual straightforward manner, though she didn't fully grasp its significance.

Root paused. His glowing eyes dimmed momentarily as if in thought before emitting a groaning response, deep and guttural.

"He says it's true," Dalia translated. "And asks if you'd like some."

Rubelle felt a spark of hope ignite within her chest. "Absolutely," she said, her voice steady despite the weight of her decision.

Root moved toward her; his towering frame surprisingly gentle in its movements. Dalia watched in fascination as he extended one massive hand over her mother's head. His long, knotted fingers pressed together, and after a moment, golden sap began to drip from the cracks in his bark.

Rubelle closed her eyes and tilted her head back, opening her mouth to catch the thick, amber liquid. The sap hit her tongue, and a burst of flavor overwhelmed her senses—a deep, earthy richness underscored by an unexpected sweetness that bloomed across her palate. Warmth followed, spreading through her throat and veins, igniting her body with vibrant energy.

She'd read about the raw potency of treant and dryad sap, how its unprocessed state could amplify mythen and enhance advanced spell work. Now, experiencing its effects firsthand, she understood its true power.

Rubelle inhaled sharply, drawing in the mythen-rich air around her and forcing it to flow violently through her body. Pain shot through her limbs as she pushed her essence to its limits, cleansing it with the raw energy coursing through her veins. Few mages dared such a reckless gamble.

Root, sensing her distress, grew anxious. He carefully picked up Dalia and cradled her, moving her to a safe distance. Rubelle gave him a grateful glance before focusing entirely on the task at hand.

Muttering under her breath, Rubelle began tracing symbols in the air with trembling fingers. The spell was both a cleansing and a healing incantation, designed to purge foreign entities from her essence. Her doubts crept in at first—was this even possible? But then a sharp pain tore through her chest, and she doubled over, gasping.

"Mama!" Dalia cried, wriggling in Root's arms, her voice thick with worry.

Rubelle's fingers clawed at the earth as tremors wracked her body. The mythen she'd forced inward now surged outward in a violent burst, her entire form trembling under its intensity.

"Get out of me!" she spat; her voice raw with desperation. She resumed her chant, forcing the cleansing spell out between shallow, labored breaths.

Voices echoed in her mind—faint at first but growing louder with each passing second.

Fool… Failure… Fail…

The sinister murmurs took on a cruel rhythm, bouncing off the trees and reverberating around them.

Root growled, holding Dalia tightly as he glanced around, his glowing eyes scanning for threats.

You cannot escape us. You will never reach the border alive.

Rubelle gritted her teeth, defying the taunts as she pushed through the agony. The voices grew louder, more menacing, until she choked, gagging violently. Something dark and vile clawed its way up her throat, and with a guttural cry, she expelled it.

Thick, writhing smoke poured from her mouth, black and malevolent, twisting in the air like living shadows.

"Mama!" Dalia screamed, tears streaming down her face as she struggled against Root's grip.

Rubelle staggered to her feet, her legs shaking beneath her weight. The vile smoke coalesced before her, forming grotesque shapes that writhed and hissed. She instinctively raised her hands, summoning the power she'd drawn from Root's sap. Mythen swirled at her fingertips, its bright hue blazing like fire as it erupted into searing flames.

The shadow was too swift. As the fiery spell surged toward it, the dark mass twisted and writhed, darting through the trees like a predator with a target in sight. Rubelle's breath hitched, and a growl escaped her lips.

"Not this time," she hissed, raising her hand. Mythen gathered in her palm, burning brighter and hotter as she poured her remaining energy into it. A blazing lance of fire erupted from her fingertips, streaking through the forest after the fleeing shadow.

The shadow's speed was unnatural, its movements erratic. It veered left, then right, slithering between the trunks and leaping over roots as if mocking her efforts. A chilling laugh echoed from all directions, sharp and guttural, crawling into her ears and burrowing into her thoughts.

"You're too slow," the voice taunted, though it was impossible to tell where it came from.

Rubelle gritted her teeth, her legs propelling her forward as she fired another burst of searing energy into the darkness. The laugh came again, louder this time, resonating like a thousand voices in unison.

"You can't stop me," it sneered, fading into the distance.

She sprinted harder, the forest around her a blur of greens and browns. Her pulse roared in her ears, matching the fiery determination burning in her chest. But no matter how fast she ran, no matter how many spells she hurled, the shadow stayed just out of reach. It darted further ahead, its sinister laughter growing fainter and fainter until—

Silence.

Rubelle skidded to a halt, her chest heaving as she looked around. The forest was still now, too still. Not even the whisper of wind moved through the leaves.

"Where are you?" she demanded, her voice breaking through the oppressive quiet. "Show yourself!"

Nothing.

She spun around, scanning the dense woods for any sign of movement. Her hands still crackled with raw energy, but her reserves were nearly drained. Finally, she let her arms fall to her sides and turned back toward Root and Dalia, her expression hard.

"We need to move. Now." Her voice was low but commanding.

Root, still holding Dalia protectively in his arms, tilted his head with a low groan. Dalia squirmed, her eyes wide with fear and confusion.

"Mama," she said softly, her voice trembling. "What… what was that? What came out of you?"

Rubelle's jaw tightened, and she looked away. "Not now, Dalia."

"But—"

"I said *not now!*" The words came out sharper than she intended. Seeing Dalia flinch, Rubelle exhaled and softened her tone. "We need to keep moving. It knows where we are now."

Dalia frowned, her gaze lingering on her mother. "It? What is *it?*"

Rubelle didn't answer. She couldn't. How could she explain what she didn't fully understand?

But she did know one thing. The evil she felt in those fleeting moments was unlike anything she had ever encountered. She prayed she would never have to face it again— but deep down, she knew that was a wish she couldn't hold onto.

"Let's go," Rubelle said firmly, motioning for Root to follow.

***

The sound of shattering glass echoed through the opulent chamber as King Charon hurled a crystal decanter across the room. The ornate vessel exploded against the far wall, its amber contents dripping down the tapestry like blood. He turned, his breath ragged, and swept a row of decorative trinkets from the polished mahogany desk with one violent motion.

The heavy wooden chair near the fireplace was his next target. He seized it by one arm and slammed it against the stone floor, the impact splitting the frame and sending splinters scattering across the rug. Charon's fists clenched, his knuckles white as he lifted the chair again and threw it against the marble column.

"Why?!" he roared, his voice raw with frustration.

He kicked at the remains of the chair, sending the fractured pieces flying, then turned his fury on the gilded mirror above the dresser. One punch, and the reflective surface cracked, its jagged lines distorting his enraged reflection.

Still, it wasn't enough.

Grabbing the edge of his desk, he heaved it over, the massive piece of furniture crashing to the floor with a deafening thud. Papers, ink, and quills spilled across the room in chaotic disarray. The act brought no relief, only a hollow ache in his chest.

Breathing heavily, Charon stared at the destruction around him. The lavish furnishings of his royal quarters now lay in ruin, their shattered remains mirroring the storm within him.

A chill ran down his spine, the familiar sensation pulling him back from the edge of his tantrum. The air grew heavy, the flickering candlelight dimming until shadows swallowed the room.

And then, it appeared.

A dark, amorphous form coalesced in the corner, its presence suffocating. The shadow's voice slithered into his ears, low and insidious.

"I see you've been keeping busy, Charon."

Charon glared at the figure, his chest heaving. "Where have you been?" he demanded.

The shadow's tone was smooth, almost amused. "Securing our interests."

"Pointless," Charon snapped, slumping onto the edge of his bed. He ran a hand through his disheveled hair, his voice trembling with frustration. "A knight reported under oath that Rubelle and her daughter were swept downriver. There's no way they survived."

He fell silent, his mind drifting to Rubelle. Her image filled his thoughts, and his heart twisted with guilt. He remembered the day he'd saved her, how he'd sworn to protect her. And now, despite everything, she was gone— lost to the currents that had taken so many before her.

His fingers dug into the fine fabric of his trousers as the pain deepened. Her daughter's fate was an even sharper dagger. To think of such innocence meeting a tragic end…

The shadow's laugh shattered his reverie, its mocking tone twisting like a dagger in his mind.

"Your compassion is touching," it taunted. "Such a big heart you have, Charon. So quick to grieve some lives while discarding others."

Charon's head snapped up, his eyes blazing with defiance. "It's not like that!" he spat. "Rubelle was like a sister to me. She was *family*!"

The shadow's voice turned cold, mocking. "Ah, yes. Family. Like the one in her chambers down the hall. The sister who dreams of slaying you, avenging your parents, *her* parents. The family you murdered."

Charon flinched at the words, his breath hitching. "It was for the greater good," he said weakly, his voice lacking conviction. "For Orivera."

The shadow's form shifted, its presence growing darker, more oppressive. It loomed over him, its voice now a menacing growl.

"Of course. For the people," it hissed. "The same people you're too afraid to tell about their new king. The people whose strongest defenders you sent to their graves."

Charon's mouth opened, but no words came. He looked down, his hands trembling.

"I didn't send them to their graves," he finally whispered. "I sent them away to buy time. To strengthen my authority—"

The shadow cut him off with a derisive snarl. "Authority? They are oath-bound, Charon. The instant they return, they will seek justice for the monarchs you butchered. Whether they desire vengeance or not, their oath demands it."

Charon paled. He was a skilled swordsman, but the thought of facing the Oath bound made his blood run cold. Their loyalty to the crown had been unshakable, their power unmatched. If they returned, there would be no escaping their wrath.

The shadow's form twisted again, its edges curling in a way that unsettled him. Though it lacked features, Charon could sense its smug satisfaction.

"You won't need to face them," it said, almost playfully. "I've already handled the Oath bound."

Charon's heart sank. "What do you mean… handled?"

The shadow didn't answer immediately, and the silence was suffocating.

Charon's mind raced, piecing together fragments of memory. The Monster March had been too small, too scattered to achieve such a feat. But then he remembered—the dark shape that had slipped through the veil when he had torn it open.

His blood turned to ice.

"No," he whispered, his voice trembling. "No, you monster. Oriana was right. You're using me. I never should have trusted you!"

The shadow moved with terrifying speed, materializing into a dark, featureless form that pinned Charon against the bed. Its grip closed around his throat, squeezing just enough to send a jolt of terror through him.

"You *dared* to summon me," it snarled, its voice like a blade scraping against stone. "You begged for this deal. We are using each other, Charon. But do not forget that you have more to lose."

Charon's hands clawed at the invisible pressure around his neck. His voice was hoarse as he choked out a plea. "I—I understand! Please… stop!"

The shadow released him, and he collapsed onto the bed, gasping for air. Though the shadow's form dissipated, its presence lingered, oppressive and cold.

"If you know so much. Then why are you still here?" Charon asked weakly, clutching at his bruised throat. "What do you want from me?"

The shadow's tone shifted, almost gleeful. "I have news," it said. "You were deceived by your knight. The mage and her spawn live."

Charon's heart skipped a beat. "What?"

"And," the shadow continued, "I know where to find them."

Charon sat up slowly, his mind spinning. He hesitated, his voice trembling as he asked, "Why didn't you tell me this sooner?"

The shadow chuckled darkly. "You didn't ask. Besides, I am bound to this domain, per our agreement. I cannot act beyond it without your permission."

Charon's lips tightened. "And if I grant you permission?"

The shadow seemed to smile, though it had no mouth. "Then I will retrieve the other half of the key for you."

Clearing his throat, Charon stood, his voice firm despite his unease. "You have my permission. Now go. Bring me that key."

"With pleasure," the shadow purred.

The room brightened as its presence faded, the oppressive darkness lifting. Charon exhaled shakily, running a hand over his face. For the first time in what felt like hours, the room was silent.

But the relief was hollow. The shadow might be gone, but its whispers lingered. Eating away at his mind like a constant reminder of their dark covenant.

***

Therion gritted his teeth, his grip tightening around the hilt of his sword as the thundering growls of the hellspawn reverberated through the ward. The translucent barrier shimmered, its surface rippling with each strike from the monstrous creatures outside.

"Lysara!" he called over his shoulder, his voice carrying the urgency of the moment. "How much longer?"

"Five more minutes!" Lysara shouted back, her hands trembling as they moved in precise, frantic gestures. She was surrounded by glowing runes etched into the stone floor, the energy from her spell climbing up the ancient pillars like serpentine trails of light. Her body began to float, suspended in a meditative trance as a soft, golden glow radiated from her.

Therion turned back to his men, their fear palpable as they gripped their weapons tightly. They didn't have five minutes. "Hold fast!" he barked, though he could see the doubt flickering in their eyes.

Suddenly, their weapons began to hum, a faint light illuminating the blades and hilts. Lysara's telepathic voice rang clear in their minds while she chanted her spell. **'*I need more time. Protect me.*'**

The knights exchanged nervous glances, and Therion saw the weight of the moment bearing down on them. He stepped forward, planting himself firmly between his men and the barrier as it flickered under the relentless assault.

"Listen to me!" Therion's voice rang out, cutting through the cacophony. "We are the vanguard of destiny! The strength of our blades and the courage in our hearts will determine whether this world stands or falls. Commander Lysara's spells gives us a chance— a chance the heavens themselves have blessed us with!"

The knights straightened, their fear replaced with a spark of determination.

"For honor," Therion continued, his voice rising, "for Orivera!"

"For Orivera!" the men echoed in unison, their voices steady now, their resolve unshaken.

A brief silence followed, filled only with the rumbling and snarling of the creatures beyond the ward. One of the knights stepped forward, he was a grey headed warrior, his armor dented and scarred, but his stance steady. He had the weathered look of a seasoned warrior.

"Commander… no, Therion Sir," he began, meeting the commander's eyes, "if this is our end, it's only right you know my name. I'm Garion of Willith. I've fought for Orivera all my life, and I'll fight to my last breath to protect it from these foul beasts."

Therion blinked, surprised but grateful. Before he could respond, another knight stepped forward. He was younger, with a boyish face that didn't match the grim determination in his eyes.

"Edrick, sir," he said. "I've always admired you. I never thought I'd fight alongside you. It's…

an honor." He swallowed hard, gripping his shield as though drawing strength from it.

The third knight was a survivor from the Emperor's hand who was already acquainted with the commander, but he gave a low chuckle, his grin almost roguish despite the circumstances. He ran a hand through his dark hair before hefting his sword.

"It's me… Kael," he said simply. "Not much for speeches, but I'll stand with you to the end."

Therion's chest tightened at the sincerity in their voices. He hadn't asked for their names, nor had he thought to learn them before now, but hearing them now felt like a bond being forged in the fires of battle. He nodded, his voice quieter but no less resolute. "Then let us fight, not as strangers, but as brothers. For Orivera, and for each other."

The ward shattered like glass.

A deafening roar erupted as the hellspawn burst through, each one an abomination of sinew, shadow, and claws. The first was a hulking beast with molten fissures running through its flesh, steam hissing with every movement. The second was serpentine, its coiled body glistening with black, chitinous armor. The third resembled a winged predator, its jagged wings slicing through the air as its glowing eyes locked onto the knights. The last was a towering humanoid with bladed limbs and a body that seemed to absorb the surrounding light.

"Hold the line!" Therion shouted as the creatures charged.

The first clash was a cacophony of steel meeting unholy flesh.

Sir Garion, the oldest of the knights, lunged at the molten beast, his blade slicing through its steaming hide. It roared, swinging a massive claw that Garion narrowly avoided. His next strike was aimed at its exposed neck, but the creature reared back, its molten blood spraying and scalding his armor.

To Garion's side, Sir Edrick faced the serpentine hellspawn. It lunged with terrifying speed, its fanged maw snapping at his shield. Edrick bashed it aside with a grunt, following up with a precise thrust to its underbelly. The creature hissed, coiling around him in a flash, its armored body squeezing until his ribs creaked and his eyes bled.

Sir Kael squared off against the winged predator, which swooped down with a shriek, its talons aiming for his throat. He rolled to the side, swinging his blade in a wide arc and severing part of its wing. The creature shrieked in fury, retaliating with a swipe that sent him sprawling, his shield splintering upon impact.

Therion faced the humanoid, its movements unnervingly calculated. It lunged with bladed arms, and he parried, sparks flying as their weapons clashed. It feinted left, then right, forcing him to stay on the defensive. Its speed was relentless, each strike faster than the last.

Garion grunted as he drove his sword into the molten beast's chest, only for its fiery blood to erupt like lava, consuming his arm and chest. He fell with a scream, the creature turning its molten eyes toward Edrick. The knight had just freed himself from the serpent's crushing coils, delivering a powerful thrust that pierced its eye. The creature writhed, hissing as it reared back. But before he could finish it off, the molten beast's claws cleaved through his torso, cutting his cry short.

Kael roared as he drove his blade into the winged predator's chest, pinning it to the ground. It screeched, slashing at him with its talons even as it bled out. He finally silenced it with a downward strike, but his victory was short-lived. The humanoid hellspawn's bladed arm pierced his back, his lifeless body crumpling to the ground before he could celebrate his victory.

Rather than turning their attention to the lone survivor, the Hellspawn seemed more consumed by their fallen kin. Their grotesque forms hunched over the carcass, ripping and tearing at it with unholy fervor. As they fed, their already monstrous bodies swelled grotesquely, sinew and muscle bulging, their shapes warping into something even more horrifying.

Therion turned to find Lysara still chanting, her voice rising in urgency. The runes surrounding her blazed wildly, pulsating with the Mythen she struggled to harness. He didn't call out to her—there was no point. He had already failed her. Failed all of them. They were the last remnants of three valiant armies reduced to ash and blood.

But he wasn't cowed.

Therion closed his eye, steadying his trembling limbs as a vision of Rubelle and Dalia flashed in his mind. He thought of their smiles, the warmth of their presence. Then, the horrifying images of what would come if these creatures reached the castle flooded his thoughts. Innocents butchered. His family torn apart.

"This ends here," he growled, his voice a broken snarl as he gripped his battered sword tighter.

The Hellspawns finally acknowledged him, their blood-slicked jaws parting to reveal jagged teeth and dripping venom. Their grotesque features were now even more menacing, their bulk nearly twice his own. They loomed over him like titans of a nightmare.

"Come at me!" Therion roared, slamming his sword against his shield.

The Molten Hellspawn charged first, a hulking monstrosity of molten rock and boiling flesh. Its weight sent tremors through the ground with every step. It swung a massive, clawed hand down at him, the air hissing as the molten heat scorched his armor. Therion dove to the side, narrowly avoiding the swipe. He rolled under its hulking form, his muscles screaming in protest. With all his strength, he thrust his sword upward, driving it into the soft, exposed flesh beneath the beast's neck. Lava spewed from the wound, searing his forearm and forcing a guttural roar from the Hellspawn.

The creature staggered, its bulk shaking the ground as it collapsed, but there was no time to celebrate.

The serpent and humanoid Hellspawn advanced next, their movements disturbingly coordinated. The serpent lunged, its fangs snapping inches from his face. Therion sidestepped, the motion awkward as fatigue weighed on his legs. He slashed at the serpent's body, leaving a deep, oozing gash. These hellspawns may have been bigger, but compared to the first they'd encountered, this battle did not feel so desperate to the Commander. The creature didn't relent and immediately tried to smash Therion to no avail.

The humanoid struck next, its bladed limb swinging with blinding speed while he was distracted. Therion managed to parry, but the sheer force sent him reeling to the ground. It lunged a gain but thankfully Therion was quick enough to grab a shield off one of the fallen's bodies to save himself. The shield absorbed the strike, but the impact left it dented and cracked. Before he could recover, the serpent coiled around his legs, yanking him off his feet and slamming him into the ground.

The air left his lungs in a ragged gasp, his ribs burning with pain. The serpent tightened its grip, its scales grinding against his armor like iron bands.

Roaring with desperate rage, Therion hacked at the coils, his muscles screaming with the effort. Dark blood sprayed as he severed the serpent's body, and it let out a shriek before falling limp. But before he could rise, the humanoid pounced. Its blade-like limb tore through his shoulder, the pain searing and blinding. Therion's vision swam, his strength faltering as he clutched at the wound. Battered and bruised he snarled as he found the two remaining Hellspawn looming over him.

Therion's breath came in shallow, ragged bursts as he forced himself to grip his sword tighter. "What are you waiting for?" he muttered, his voice laced with defiance even as his body trembled with exhaustion.

The Hellspawns had already started moving in for the kill, and Therion had made peace with his Goddess, when just as suddenly, they froze.

Their heads turned sharply, as if hearing a sound only they could perceive. The humanoid tilted its head, its featureless face twitching.

And then, without warning, they melted into the shadows, their forms dissipating like smoke.

Therion blinked, his vision blurring as he stared at the spot where they had stood. The silence that followed was deafening.

His legs gave out, and he collapsed onto his knees. Blood dripped from his wounds, pooling around him as his grip on his sword loosened. Just before darkness claimed him, he felt a shift in the air. A spiral of light erupted in the center of the circle of runes Lysara had conjured. The radiance of it was blinding, swirling upward as several figures emerged from its depths.

He barely registered the golden glow or the faint outline of armor and flowing robes before his head met the ground with a dull thud. Though he hadn't felt the fall, his body was numb and his mind was drifting away.

"Therion!" He heard Lysara's voice call, distant but urgent. He caught a glimpse of her over him bathed in the light, but he could not make out what she was saying before everything went black.

***

Rubelle's breath caught as the border finally came into view. A shimmering expanse of light marked the edge of the Fairy Woods, a stretch of no man's land that marked the beginning of the Mythenian territories. Relief blossomed in her chest, and she clutched the gem hidden beneath her cloak, her fingers trembling. "I've done it, Princess," she whispered to herself, a fleeting smile tugging at her lips. She sent a silent prayer for the princess's safety, her heart aching with the hope that her mission had not been in vain.

One she'd crossed over the order, she was more than certain that everything would be right with the world. Unbeknownst to her, Charon and the fallen would not allow it. The shadow's sinister presence watched from the top of a hill. The air chilled as the dark figure observed first admired its form, with every passing day it grew more defined, more flesh and blood than apparition. Its voice was a low, guttural growl, carrying an order that echoed with malice.

The darkness spread like ink spilling across the forest floor, twisting and writhing until it coalesced into three hulking forms. The hellspawns rose, their grotesque shapes barely constrained by their sinewy, shifting flesh. The shadow grimaced, it could have sworn that in the window of the rift being open it'd summoned more hellspawns than this— nonetheless, it felt confident that this number would be enough.

Find the key. Kill the Lessers.

Its dark voice ordered and without hesitation, the hellspawns charged toward Rubelle and her daughter.

Root was the first to feel the disturbance. The Treant paused and stared back as birds fled from the trees and the sky itself darkened ominously. The treant groaned and growled, his massive body stiffening as it turned away from the path.

"Root?" Rubelle called, her voice edged with concern. "What is it?"

Dalia clung to her mother, her wide eyes darting between the treant and the encroaching darkness. "He says… something horrible is coming," she translated, her voice trembling.

Root let out a deep, resonant groan and turned to face the direction of the oncoming threat. That's when the familiar skin crawling sensation of evil washed over her. 'It's here….' She paled at the realization. Root took a heavy step forward, his roots cracking the earth as he moved.

"No! Root, don't!" Dalia cried, breaking free from her mother's grasp and running toward him. Rubelle rushed forward, grabbing her daughter and holding her tightly

"Dalia, no!" she said, her voice firm despite the fear in her heart.

"He's saying he'll fight it. He's asking us to leave!" Tears streamed down Dalia's face as she struggled against her mother's grip. "Mummy tell him he's wrong. Tell him he's going to get hurt!"

Rubelle hesitated as the Treant gave her a stern gaze.

She didn't need to speak its language to understand its intentions. Rubelle felt her very being tremble. She hadn't even laid eyes on the creatures yet, but the oppressive weight in the air was enough to make her knees weak. She nodded to Root, her voice shaking as she said, "Thank you, Root. Thank you."

"Mummy?" Dalia queried in bewilderment as Rubelle swept her off her feet and carried her along against her pleas. The treant groaned low in acknowledgment, his glowing amber eyes softening briefly before he lumbered back toward the threat. "Mummy NO! Bad mummy! Put me down!"

Rubelle held Dalia tightly, her heart heavy as she darted toward the border, desperate to make it past while they still could.

While they fled, Root marched up to a path he knew their pursuers would have to take. It was a clearing, the now darkened forest opening into a broad space filled with jagged rocks and mossy terrain. He planted his massive feet into the ground, his body towering like a living fortress as he manifested thorns on either side of the path like a barrier. And then he waited.

A moment later, the hellspawns emerged from the shadow of the trees before him.

The first was a hulking brute with molten cracks coursing through its flesh, steam hissing with every movement. The second was a serpentine monstrosity, its body armored in jagged black scales. The third was an elongated, nightmarish predator, its limbs unnaturally long, and its claws scraping the earth with an ear-piercing screech.

They paused, observing the treant, their glowing eyes assessing their target. This was the first mythenian they were facing since they were brought into this world, and they were intelligent enough to understand that it was not a creature they should underestimate. They found themselves in a staring contested that lasted seconds, but felt like an eternity.

The brute roared first, charging forward with earth-shaking steps. Root let out a deep, resonant growl and met the creature head-on.

The impact of thick bark slamming against a thick wall of darkness given flesh was thunderous. As Root slammed his bulk into the brute it sent shockwaves through the ground. His massive fists, each like a battering ram, crashed down onto the hellspawn, driving it into the earth as he utilized his innate gifts of nature with no need for chants. Vines erupted from his body, snaking around the brute's limbs and dragging it closer as Root pummeled it with unrelenting force. But Root had not noticed that no matter how hard or brutally he beat the monster, its wounds seemed to stitch right back together the very next instant.

The serpentine hellspawn darted to the side, attempting to bypass the treant and its wall of thorns, but Root's roots shot out as spikes, piercing its flank and pinning it in place. The elongated predator leapt forward, its claws aimed at the treant's back. Claws that could have easily cut down trees ripped through the treant's flesh as sap smeared over the floor. Root roared, twisting with surprising speed, and swatted it away with a massive branch-like arm. The predator crashed into the trees, but before Root could follow up, the brute surged forward again, slamming its fiery fists into Root's side.

Roots erupted from the ground, coiling around the brute and dragging it back as Root turned his attention to the other two. He stomped toward the serpentine creature, his massive foot crushing the ground as he drove his roots deeper into its body.

But the hellspawns were relentless. The predator darted back in, its claws slicing into Root's bark with horrifying precision. The molten brute broke free of the vines and slammed its fists into Root's chest, each blow splintering bark and sending shards flying.

Root roared, his voice echoing through the forest like a mourning bell.

Rubelle ran and didn't stop or turn until they'd made it past the border and a good mile into the Fairy Woods. Dalia clutched her mother's cloak, sobbing uncontrollably.

"He's hurting, Mama! I can hear them hurting him!" she cried.

Rubelle froze, her heart shattering at her daughter's words. She had done everything to ensure they reached the border, but now Root's cries echoed in her soul. She looked back at the shimmering boundary, the sanctuary they had worked so hard to reach. Yet her feet felt heavy as she stood there, torn between safety and the debt she owed the treant.

"Now what?" she whispered to herself the instant they crossed the border, her voice hollow with confusion. Dalia's sobs grew louder, her small hands gripping her mother's cloak.

Rubelle hesitated. When she'd come here she'd expected some sign or miracle, anything to prove that she'd done the right thing running as her Princess had instructed her. But now she was standing on foreign soil, cradling her crying daughter while a new found ally was sacrificing themselves for her sake a short mile away.

'Dear Goddess…' Rubelle inhaled sharply as she finally came to a decision.

Kneeling, she pressed the treasure she carried into Dalia's hands. "I want you to find a tree, and wait under it for me. Only me." she said, her voice trembling but firm. "Don't make a sound, do move, only wait for me. No matter what happens."

Dalia looked up at her, wide-eyed. "Mama, no—"

"I'll save your friend." Rubelle cupped her daughter's face, forcing a reassuring smile. "And I'll be back. I swear it."

Dalia sniffled, but nodded. She knew her mother meant every word, and she believed in her. Closing her eyes Rubelle muttered a quick spell, a dull shimmer of protective mythen enveloped Dalia when she finished. Standing, she planted a kiss on her forehead and turned. "Find a tree. Stay safe. And wait for me."

"I will." Dalia assured her, running deeper into the forest to do as she was instructed. Rubelle took a deep breath and stepped back from the border. Although she had no received the sign she'd hoped for, crossing the border was not in vain. The mythen in the air on the other side was so dense the power she felt flow naturally around her made her skin tingle.

In the brief moment the mother daughter duo were away, the clearing Root had chosen had become a battlefield. The Treant was battered and missing an arm, yet stood surrounded by the three hellspawns. His body trembled with exhaustion, and it grumbled over how unfair it was that his assailant's wounds simply glossed over.

The hellspawns were exhausted.

He'd pushed them as fair as any creature could without the proper knowledge of how they were slain. One of them lunged at him in an attack that would have been fatal, but the instant it did, its mouth was suddenly forced shut by a blast of flame that sent it skidding back. 'You'd done well, friend.' Rubelle thought proudly as she summoned a wall of fire between Root and the hellspawns, momentarily halting their advance.

Root turned, his amber eyes widening in relief as he saw Rubelle emerge from the forest, her hands blazing with magic. "You made my daughter cry," she said, her voice shaking with both fear and fury. "You owe her an apology."

The treant groaned what she hoped was a witty comeback, but she had no way of knowing without her little translator being there. She caught a glimpse of the horrors, their grotesque beings frightened her so much she was almost tempted to run away. She swallowed her fear and paled as she hoped her fire would hold.

The hellspawns hesitated at the flames, but one leapt through, its molten form ignoring the heat. "Damn it!" Rubelle cursed under her breath as she intensified the wall of fire behind it, keeping the other two at bay, while she and Root faced the charging brute.

The battle was vicious. Root's remaining arm slammed into the brute, while Rubelle's spells bombarded it with light. But the creature was relentless, landing a heavy blow that sent Rubelle sprawling.

Root roared in fury, his roots spearing through the brute's body and slamming it to the ground. It thrashed violently, and Rubelle, clutching her injured side, summoned her remaining strength to deliver the final blow— a searing burst of magic that left the hellspawn smoldering.

The other two hellspawns watched from the edge of the fire, their glowing eyes calculating.

Rubelle leaned against Root, her magic waning. "Why aren't they attacking?" she muttered.

The air grew colder.

Her heart sank as the familiar chill crept over her, and she realized the truth.

"The gem," she whispered, her voice laced with dread.

"Dalia!" she screamed, spinning toward the border.

But almost on cue the hellspawns surged forward, determined to deter their efforts long enough for them to seize the key from the now alone and defenseless child in the fairy woods.

Chapter Ten: A Miracle/The Blessed

Therion awoke with a sharp gasp, his body jolting upright only to be pulled back down by a wave of searing pain. He groaned, his vision swimming as he blinked against the soft, natural light filtering into the room. The space around him was modest but comforting. Smooth wooden walls, crafted with the precision and artistry of nature itself, surrounded him. There was no need for excessive decoration; the grain of the wood alone was beautiful, telling stories of growth and age. A faint, pleasant scent of pine and fresh herbs filled the air, mingling with the earthy aroma of damp soil.

The bed he lay on was sturdy yet soft, its frame seemingly grown rather than built, with sheets woven from a fabric that felt both delicate and durable. A small table sat beside him, holding a steaming cup of something herbal and a shallow dish of salve. Light streamed in through a lattice of wooden slats, dappled with the greens and golds of the leaves outside.

The door creaked open softly, and a figure entered. He was tall and lean, his movements graceful yet deliberate. His sharp, angular features were framed by silver hair tied back neatly, and his eyes—large, luminous, and inquisitive—seemed to take in every detail at once. He was unmistakably Mythenian, his very presence exuding an air of ancient wisdom and calm.

"Ah, you're awake," the Mythenian said, his voice soft yet carrying an unmistakable authority. "How do you feel?"

Therion tried to respond, his throat dry and voice hoarse. "I'm… fine." He winced as he tried to push himself up, a sharp pain radiating from his side. A groan escaped him despite his efforts to hold it in.

The Mythenian stepped closer, placing a steadying hand on his shoulder. "Easy now," he said gently. "You have several broken bones and lacerations. Your body… did not respond well to our healing magic. You mustn't push yourself too quickly."

Therion's brow furrowed as fragments of his last memories resurfaced. "The others…" he rasped, fear tightening his chest. "What about the others?"

The Mythenian's expression darkened, and he hesitated. "By the time we arrived, it was too late for them."

Therion's eyes widened in horror. "No…" He shook his head, his voice breaking. "No! They can't be… Lysara! Where is she? Tell me she's alive!"

The Mythenian's frown deepened, his gaze heavy with sorrow. "Lysara gave the last of her strength to ensure you were in our care. She… she spoke of her faith in you."

Therion's chest tightened as he recalled the frail whisper of her voice, the memory of her trembling hand on his as she made him promise to survive. His body trembled as he staggered back, nearly collapsing again onto the bed. The Mythenian caught him, his grip firm yet compassionate.

"You are safe here," the Mythenian assured him. "We will care for you as long as you need."

Therion shook his head, his mind racing. The faces of his companions flashed before him, the weight of their loss pressing down on him. Yet one thought burned brighter than the rest. "My family," he said hoarsely, gripping the Mythenian's arm. "I have family in the capital. My wife, my daughter. I need to see them. They need to know I'm alive."

The Mythenian's expression grew serious. "We know what is happening in the capital," he said gravely. "It is not safe for you to return there. I fear we cannot, in good conscience, allow it."

Therion's voice rose, tinged with desperation. "Please! If I can't go to them, let me see them. Even if it's through some mirror, something! They have to know I'm well."

The Mythenian hesitated, studying him carefully. Finally, he nodded. "A father's worry is not to be ignored," he said. "Follow me closely."

Therion swung his legs over the side of the bed, grimacing as pain shot through his body. With the Mythenian's support, he managed to stand and steady himself. Together, they stepped out of the room into the open air.

Therion's breath caught in his throat as he took in the sight before him. The settlement was a marvel, a harmonious blend of nature and craftsmanship. Towering trees, their trunks wide enough to house entire rooms, formed the foundation of the village. Wooden walkways and bridges connected the trees, their railings carved with intricate patterns that seemed to hum faintly with latent Mythen. Homes and workshops were seamlessly integrated into the natural architecture, their roofs covered in moss and flowering vines. The air was thick with the energy of the Mythen, a gentle hum that resonated with his very being.

Villagers moved gracefully along the walkways, their features unmistakably Mythenian. They carried baskets of herbs, tended to glowing crystal lamps, or sat in quiet contemplation. Though Therion's presence was clearly an anomaly, they paid him no mind, going about their day with quiet purpose.

The Mythenian led him across a curved bridge toward a central structure, its design more elaborate than the others. As they walked, Therion couldn't help but marvel at the serenity of the place, though his heart ached with worry for his family.

"This way," the Mythenian said, guiding him through a beautifully arched doorway. Inside, the air grew warmer, and Therion's chest tightened with anticipation.

Therion followed his Mythenian guide down a winding corridor carved from living wood, its surfaces glowing faintly with a bioluminescent hue. The air was fragrant, a blend of pine and wildflowers, and his footsteps were muted on the soft, mossy ground. The path opened into a grand chamber, its ceiling soaring high with branches intertwining to form natural arches, illuminated by suspended orbs of light. At the center stood a circular table surrounded by several elder Mythenians, each radiating an aura of ancient wisdom.

Therion's guide bowed deeply before the council, his posture reverent. Therion, despite the weight of his injuries and grief, mimicked the gesture with as much respect as he could muster. The elders turned their sharp, owlish gazes toward them, their expressions a mixture of curiosity and gravity.

The elder at the head of the table, a woman whose silver hair flowed like a river down her back, spoke first. "We sense urgency in your arrival. Speak, Valdion."

Valdion, Therion's guide, straightened and addressed the assembly. "Esteemed elders, this is Therion, the sole survivor we took in a day ago. He has requested our assistance in confirming the well-being of his kin. He believes they remain in the capital, and his worry is profound."

Therion stiffened at the revelation. **A day?** He'd been unconscious for a full day? He kept his expression neutral, unwilling to show weakness in this moment, and listened intently as the elders deliberated.

One of the elders, a woman with deep crimson markings streaking her cheeks and sharp emerald eyes, sighed heavily. "The mage Lysara… she was no different from kin to us. Her loss is a wound we feel deeply." A ripple of somber agreement passed through the council.

Another elder, a broad-shouldered man with golden accents running along his ash-grey skin, interrupted, his voice clipped and tense. "We acknowledge the debt owed to her, but our people face dire matters. The rift is threatening to unravel, and a great evil looms on the horizon."

The mention of the rift sent murmurs through the chamber, the weight of their shared concern palpable. He continued, his voice rising.

"With the realm of man threatening the balance, our safest course is to seal off our borders entirely."

The eldest among them, seated at the center, nodded slowly. Her amber eyes glimmered with wisdom as she folded her hands atop the table. "You speak wisely. Valdion, we must decline your request."

Before the words could fully settle, Therion stepped forward, his body protesting the sudden movement. "Forgive my intrusion, elders," he began, bowing again, "but I must speak."

The council exchanged glances before the eldest gestured for him to continue.

Therion took a steadying breath. "This evil you speak of… I have seen it. For the past three days, it has hunted me and slain my men. It came from beyond the rift."

Gasps and alarmed whispers erupted among the council. Some elders exchanged looks of disbelief, while others immediately began arguing about the possibility of such a thing.

A third elder, her features marked by delicate, iridescent scales and a crown of braided silver hair, leaned forward. Her voice was calm but insistent. "You are certain of this?"

Therion met her gaze. "I am. I saw it with my own eyes. Ferocious hellspawn, but they are vulnerable to mythen. It is the only thing that can hold them at bay."

His words sparked renewed discussion, some elders appearing deeply unsettled while others pressed for more details. Amid the chaos, Therion's voice rose again, resolute and impassioned. "I've lost too many people to run from this. My family… they are my only reason to fight. Let me see them.

Let them know I am well. After that, I swear to stand with you against this threat."

The chamber fell silent at his declaration. The elders regarded him with a mixture of respect and uncertainty. Finally, the eldest leaned forward, her piercing gaze locking onto his. "You would fight alongside us? Against an enemy you barely understand?"

Therion straightened, ignoring the pain in his ribs. "On my oath, I will. If it means protecting my family and ensuring their safety, I will fight."

Valdion, standing beside him, smiled faintly, his pride evident. The eldest leaned back in her chair, the lines of her face softening slightly. "So be it. Valdion, take him to the Grand Mirror."

A collective murmur of approval passed through the council. Valdion gestured for Therion to follow, and the two left the chamber.

Valdion led Therion through another set of intricately carved doors, their surfaces etched with glowing runes that pulsed faintly as they passed. Therion's mind was still heavy with the image of his family, safe but vulnerable, their faces etched with fear. Yet, he forced himself to focus, following Valdion's confident stride.

They entered a chamber unlike any Therion had ever seen. It was cavernous, the air charged with an almost electric hum. At its center stood a massive mirror, its frame carved from a single piece of pale wood that seemed to radiate an inner light. The surface of the mirror shimmered, catching Therion's breath in his throat. At first, it seemed solid, like polished silver, but as he approached, he noticed the faint undulation of its surface, as though it were liquid contained within an impossibly thin membrane.

Therion instinctively halted, eyes narrowing. "What is this?" he asked, his voice barely above a whisper.

Valdion turned to face him, a faint smile softening his otherwise stern features. "This, Therion, is the Grand Mirror. It is a treasure from the Era of Mythen, a relic of our ancestors' ingenuity and connection to the mythen that binds all realms."

Therion stepped closer, his boots muffled by the soft moss lining the chamber floor. "It doesn't look like any mirror I've seen."

"Because it isn't," Valdion said, reverently brushing his fingers along the mirror's frame. "Its purpose goes far beyond reflection. It can channel the essence of other mirrors and offer glimpses of distant places. But its true power lies in its ability to find and connect with anyone, anywhere, regardless of their destination."

Therion's eyes widened. "Then you're saying... it can find my family?"

Valdion nodded solemnly. "Indeed. It is most often used to communicate between tribes or oversee our territories. But for one such as you, with a bond so strong, it can surely locate those you seek."

The Mythenian gestured for Therion to stand before the mirror. "Place your hand upon its surface and focus on the one you wish to find. Speak their name if it helps. The mythen will do the rest."

Therion hesitated for a moment, then stepped forward, raising a hand to the shimmering surface. It felt cool and oddly pliant beneath his touch, like pressing against the skin of a water bubble. He closed his eyes, inhaling deeply.

"Rubelle," he whispered, the name carrying the weight of his love and desperation.

The mirror responded instantly. Its surface rippled and shimmered, colors swirling like an iridescent storm. Therion opened his eyes as the chaos settled, forming a clear image. There she was—Rubelle, alive and moving, her face drawn but determined. His heart leapt at the sight, but his relief was short-lived.

"Rubelle!" Valdion exclaimed softly, his surprise breaking Therion's focus.

Therion turned sharply to him. "You know her?"

Valdion's eyes narrowed, his expression growing serious. "Rubelle, like Lysara, was once my student. But she… she's in trouble."

Therion's gaze snapped back to the mirror. Rubelle was no longer alone. A towering treant, its bark-like skin shifting as it moved, stood beside her. Though imposing, it did not seem hostile. But then the image shifted, revealing a pack of hellspawn closing in from the shadows. The sight sent a jolt of terror through Therion's body.

"No," he muttered, his voice shaking. "No, no, no!"

The mirror's image began to blur and shift again, the colors darkening. Suddenly, another figure appeared. It was Dalia, cradling something small and radiant, though the mirror's surface blurred the object, shrouding it in a blinding light.

Valdion's brow furrowed as he leaned closer. "What is she holding?"

Therion's voice was hoarse. "I don't know. But that's my daughter. But… I don't know where they are."

Before either could speak further, the mirror's surface darkened completely, a suffocating blackness filling the image. A sudden force burst outward, sending Therion stumbling backward. He caught himself, but the tremor in his limbs betrayed his fear.

Valdion's expression was grim. "That... that should not happen. The Grand Mirror does not fail. Something... something evil is after your child."

Therion's breathing quickened. "I need to help them! Tell me where they are!"

Valdion's gaze softened, but his voice remained steady. "They are near the Border, within the Fairy Forest. I recognize its mists and trees. But... the journey is perilous, and time is against us."

Therion clenched his fists. "Then I'll go alone. Just tell me how to get there."

Valdion shook his head, already turning toward the door. "No. You will not go unprepared. Wait here."

Moments later, Valdion returned, carrying a set of enchanted leather armor and Therion's sword. The armor's surface gleamed faintly, runes etched into its surface glowing with latent power. He handed it to Therion, muttering a spell under his breath. As the incantation ended, the runes flared briefly, then settled into a steady glow.

"This armor will protect you," Valdion said firmly, "and these runes will strengthen your resilience against the dark forces you'll face. Your sword has also been blessed. It should serve you well."

Therion donned the armor quickly, its weight surprisingly light yet sturdy. He took the sword, feeling a hum of energy resonate through the hilt. "Thank you, Valdion."

The Mythenian placed a hand on his shoulder. "Save your thanks for when you return."

Valdion moved to the Grand Mirror, his hands weaving intricate patterns in the air as he chanted. The mirror's surface began to shimmer violently, glowing with an intensity that filled the chamber. The hum of magic grew louder, a palpable force pressing against Therion's skin. He recognized the energy—it was the same spell Lysara had used to summon him to the frosted peaks.

The mirror's surface surged with light, forming a swirling portal. Valdion turned to Therion, his expression resolute. "The path is open. Go, and may the mythen guide you."

Therion nodded, steeling himself. His grip on the sword tightened as he stepped toward the portal. The light enveloped him, and for a moment, he felt the familiar pull of magic, the disorienting rush of being transported.

Then, with a final breath, he leapt into the unknown, determined to save his family no matter the cost.

***

Root groaned, his massive, bark-covered body sagging under the weight of his injuries. Splinters jutted from gashes along his limbs, and sap seeped from deep wounds. He leaned heavily on one remaining arm, the others hanging limp at his sides. Rubelle wasn't faring much better. She knelt a few paces away, her chest heaving as she fought to stay conscious. The ground beneath her shimmered faintly with spent mythen, evidence of the energy she'd poured into her attacks. Her ears rang, and her limbs felt as if they were weighed down by iron chains. Despite her efforts, the hellspawn stood undeterred, their grotesque forms knitting themselves back together with terrifying efficiency.

Rubelle's mind raced, searching desperately for some opening, some strategy that could turn the tide. Her fingers curled around the hilt of her dagger, though she knew it would do little against these creatures. One of the hellspawn, its eyes glowing like embers, locked onto her. It crouched low, its sinewy frame coiling like a spring, ready to pounce.

Then the world erupted in light.

Rubelle's head jerked up, her breath catching in her throat as a brilliant flash tore through the oppressive darkness above them. For a moment, the hellspawn hesitated, their predatory snarls faltering as they too turned their attention skyward.

The reprieve was fleeting. One of the creatures darted forward, taking advantage of Rubelle's distraction. She tried to move, but her body refused to respond. Her heart shattered as she realized she wouldn't be able to stop it. The hellspawn lunged, its claws glinting as it closed the gap.

"Stay away from my wife!"

A furious roar echoed through the clearing, and the hellspawn's momentum was abruptly halted as a blade, glowing with etched runes, cleaved through its arm. The severed limb hit the ground with a sickening thud, and the creature tumbled forward, howling in pain.

Rubelle's vision blurred with tears as she saw the man standing between her and the creature. "Therion!" she cried, her voice breaking with equal parts relief and disbelief.

Therion spared her a brief, pained smile, his sword already raised defensively. "Rubelle, Dalia is in danger," he said, his voice urgent but steady. "Go to her. I'll handle this."

Rubelle's heart clenched. She wanted to argue, to stay and fight by his side, but she could see the fire in his eyes. He wasn't asking— he was pleading. She nodded, swallowing the lump in her throat. "Be careful," she whispered before forcing herself to her feet. With a last, lingering glance at him, she turned and darted away, each step a painful reminder of her depleted strength.

Root groaned again, dragging himself upright. The treant's towering form cast a protective shadow over Therion. "Protect..." he growled, his deep voice resonating with the earth itself.

Therion squared his shoulders, feeling a flicker of relief. He wasn't alone. "Let's end this," he muttered, gripping his sword tightly.

The hellspawn snarled in unison, their eyes burning with malevolence. They moved as one, their forms a blur of dark, sinewy flesh. Root swung a massive arm, his bark-covered fist crashing into one of the creatures with enough force to send it skidding across the ground. The impact splintered his arm further, but the treant didn't falter.

Therion darted forward, his sword a blur as he met the second hellspawn head-on. Their claws raked against his blade, sparks flying with each clash. One managed to slash across his side, and he gritted his teeth against the pain, countering with a swift upward strike that split its torso. The creature shrieked, but even as its body collapsed, it began to knit itself back together.

"Mythen!" Therion shouted, remembering Valdion's words. He focused, channeling his will into the runes on his blade. The etchings flared to life, and his next strike seared through the hellspawn's regenerating form. This time, it stayed down, its body dissolving into ash.

Root let out a triumphant roar as he pinned another hellspawn beneath his massive foot. His other arm, weakened and splintered, still managed to slam down with enough force to crush the creature's skull. But the effort took its toll. The treant staggered, his movements slowing.

"Behind you!" Therion shouted, rushing to intercept the third hellspawn as it leapt toward Root's exposed back. His blade met its claws mid-air, deflecting the attack. The creature's momentum carried them both to the ground, and Therion gasped as his shoulder struck a jagged rock.

The hellspawn loomed over him, its fangs bared in a grotesque grin. Therion twisted, driving his knee into its abdomen to force it off. He rolled to his feet, swinging his blade in a wide arc. The creature dodged, its movements unnervingly fast, but Root's intervention came like a thunderclap. The treant's arm swept through the air, catching the hellspawn and hurling it into a nearby tree with a sickening crunch.

"Good work," Therion panted, giving Root a brief nod. Blood dripped from a gash on his forehead, stinging his eyes, but he forced himself to focus as he darted after the hellspawn, driving his blade thr9ugh its head before it could heal.

The final hellspawn rose, its body mangled but still moving. It hissed, a sound filled with rage and desperation, before retreating into the shadows.

Therion's chest heaved as he scanned the darkness, waiting for it to strike again. But the forest remained still, the oppressive silence broken only by the distant sound of Rubelle's hurried footsteps fading away.

Root groaned, sagging against a nearby tree. 'Gone… for now,' the treant thought wearily.

Therion nodded approvingly at the creature, his grip on his sword loosening. His adrenaline was fading, and the pain of his injuries began to set in. He turned toward the direction Rubelle had gone, determination hardening his expression. "I have to catch up with her," he said, his voice hoarse.

He took a step, then another, his body protesting with every movement. His vision swam, the edges darkening as blood loss and exhaustion took their toll. He stumbled, forcing himself forward through sheer will. But as he neared the border, his legs gave out. He collapsed to the ground, his sword slipping from his grasp.

***

Dalia sat huddled beneath an ancient tree she felt would be too difficult for her mother to spot. Her small hands trembled as they cradled the gem she'd been tasked with. The stone pulsed faintly, an ethereal, shifting light swirling within its depths like liquid fire. It was not just beautiful— it felt alive, resonating with a heartbeat that matched her own. The surface shimmered, iridescent and hypnotic, with colors that seemed to flow into one another like molten glass. Her grandmother had called it a relic of their lineage, a key to something far greater than they could comprehend. Yet, in Dalia's tiny hands, it felt impossibly heavy, as though she held the weight of the entire realm.

She closed her eyes tightly, clutching the gem to her chest. Her whispered prayer to the Goddess O'Rivera was shaky but earnest. "Please, protect Mama. Protect us all."

A chill crept over her, and the soft whispers of the wind twisted into sinister murmurs. Dalia's eyes snapped open as shadows began pooling at the edges of the clearing. The darkness slithered forward, snuffing out the light around her. She whimpered, backing against the tree, her wide eyes darting as the shadows grew taller, darker, until they formed a towering figure that loomed over her like a storm cloud.

"Do not fear, child," a voice purred, smooth and chilling. The shadow leaned closer, its form undefined but menacing, its hand-like appendage stretching toward her. "Give me what you hold, little one. It is not meant for your hands."

Dalia clutched the gem tighter, shaking her head furiously. "No! It's mine!"

The voices multiplied, hissing and snapping like a chorus of serpents. "Foolish child. Kill her. Take it."

Tears streamed down her cheeks as she squeezed her eyes shut. She pressed the gem to her heart and whispered her prayer louder, her voice trembling. The shadow laughed, a cruel, hollow sound that made her shiver. "Brave, aren't you?" it taunted. "But bravery will not save you. You have no choice."

Suddenly, a voice rang out, fierce and desperate. "Don't touch my daughter!"

Dalia's eyes flew open. "Mama!" she cried, seeing Rubelle sprinting toward them, her face etched with determination and fury. Relief flooded Dalia's chest, but it was short-lived. The darkness swirled around her feet, snaring her legs and rooting her in place. She screamed as the shadows rose higher, enveloping her like a black tide.

"Dalia!" Rubelle's voice was muffled as the darkness thickened, forming an impenetrable barrier between them.

Inside the void, Dalia was trapped in silence save for the voices that clawed at her mind. "Give us the key," one growled, low and threatening. Another hissed, "There is no escape. Surrender it!"

She sobbed, trembling as she clutched the gem tighter. Her prayer faltered, her voice quivering. Then, amidst the oppressive blackness, a soft glow appeared. A single butterfly of pure light fluttered into view, its wings shimmering with vibrant colors that painted the darkness with streaks of hope.

Dalia gasped, her tears momentarily forgotten. It was the same butterfly she had seen in the market, the one her grandmother had called a blessing. The light it radiated was warm, soothing, and impossibly bright. The voices recoiled, hissing in anger, but Dalia felt a surge of courage. She reached out, her tiny hand trembling, and touched the butterfly.

In an instant, the butterfly erupted in a blinding pillar of light that shot skyward, tearing through the darkness. The shadows shrieked as they disintegrated, consumed by the light. The void around Dalia shattered like glass, revealing the world outside. She hovered several feet above the ground, unconscious, her small body enveloped in a radiant glow.

Rubelle staggered back, shielding her eyes from the brilliance. The light collided with the dark veil that had surrounded the clearing, and instead of an explosive clash, there was a soothing hum. The air shimmered with a myriad of colors, streaking across the sky like shooting stars in broad daylight.

Rubelle's wounds began to close, the pain ebbing away as the light washed over her. She stared in awe, her breath caught in her throat. "Dalia…" she whispered, daring to look into the light.

At the heart of it, she saw her daughter, cradled in the warm glow, safe and unharmed. But the light was not just light. It was taking shape, forming a figure that was both majestic and serene. It was a stag, radiant and graceful, yet there was something distinctly feminine about its presence. When it spoke, its voice was neither loud nor soft, but it resonated deep within her soul.

"Rubelle Wynters."

Rubelle fell to her knees, overwhelmed by the presence. Her body trembled, not in fear but in reverence. Tears streamed down her face as she recognized the being before her. "Goddess O'Rivera," she breathed, her voice barely audible.

The goddess regarded her with an expression that was both kind and resolute. "I have watched over this world for eons, but I have been absent for too long. Through your courage and faith, you have granted me this opportunity to intervene in my son's wrongdoings."

Rubelle's mind swirled with questions, but one rose above the rest. She dared to lift her gaze. "Why me?" she asked, her voice cracking. "Why my family?"

O'Rivera's gaze softened. "Because I have seen your heart, Rubelle. Your will, your love, and your resolve. You are stronger than you know, and it is that strength that will carry you through the trials ahead."

The goddess's expression grew somber. "The path before you will be fraught with darkness. But know this: you are no longer alone. Believe in my word, and you will find the strength to prevail."

The light began to fade, and Dalia gently floated downward, settling into her mother's arms. Rubelle cradled her daughter tightly, her tears falling freely as relief and gratitude overwhelmed her.

"Mama," Dalia murmured faintly, her tiny hand clutching her mother's shirt.

Rubelle pressed a kiss to her daughter's forehead. "I'm here, my love. I'm here."

Footsteps echoed behind her, and Rubelle turned sharply, her body tense with fear. Her eyes widened in shock as she saw Therion standing there, battered and bloodied but alive. He staggered toward them, his eyes filled with relief and love.

"Rubelle. Dalia," he rasped, his voice thick with emotion.

Rubelle's tears flowed anew as he dropped to his knees and pulled them both into his arms. They clung to each other, a family reunited against all odds.

Eleven: Cursed

The air was heavy with the scent of pine and earth, a stillness settling over the clearing as the angelic voices of the Forest Mythenians rose in haunting harmony. The ethereal melody wove through the towering trees, their trunks glimmering faintly as if attuned to the solemn ritual. Soft, golden light filtered through the canopy, painting the scene in a mournful glow. In the center of the circle, Lysara's body lay atop a carefully arranged bed of hay and fragrant herbs. She was clad in ceremonial armor, her sword placed reverently upon her chest, the hilt cradled by her lifeless hands. The blade gleamed faintly, a reminder of her strength and sacrifice.

The fire that consumed her was no ordinary flame.

It was conjured by spell craft, its glow beginning as a flicker of silver-blue at her feet.

Slowly, the flames grew, dancing upward in tendrils that shimmered with iridescent hues, consuming the hay and herbs with a deliberate, almost sacred patience. Sparks rose into the air like fireflies, and with each moment, the fire seemed to pulse in harmony with the choir's hymn, as though the very essence of the forest grieved her loss.

Therion stood apart from the others, his broad shoulders squared as he watched the flames take hold. His face was stern, but the tightness in his jaw betrayed his grief. He felt a profound sense of gratitude for Lysara's sacrifice, though it warred with the guilt of her loss. Without her, he doubted he would still be alive to stand here, let alone protect his family. The ache in his heart was a deep, gnawing wound, but he let no tears fall. Not yet.

A soft rustle drew his attention, and he turned to see Rubelle stepping into the clearing. The dress the Mythenians had given her was unlike anything he'd seen before. It was a deep emerald hue that shimmered with hints of gold when the light touched it, the fabric flowing like water around her as she moved. Intricate patterns of vines and leaves were embroidered along the hem and sleeves, emphasizing the grace of her movements. Her auburn hair, loosely braided, framed her face in soft waves that caught the golden light.

For a moment, Therion forgot his sorrow. His lips parted as his gaze traveled over her, taking in the sight of the woman who had fought beside him, suffered beside him, and now stood radiant before him. "You're beautiful," he murmured, his voice rough with emotion.

Rubelle's eyes softened, and she crossed the distance between them, her hand reaching up to cup his cheek. Without a word, she pulled him into a deep, lingering kiss. It was a kiss that spoke of love, of relief, and of the strength they drew from each other. When they parted, she rested her forehead against his, her voice barely above a whisper. "I still can't believe she's gone."

Therion's gaze drifted back to the flames. "She was a powerful mage," he said. "Without her, I wouldn't have made it. None of us would have." His fists clenched at his sides. "I regret that I couldn't honor them properly. All of them."

Before Rubelle could respond, a steady voice broke through the melody of the choir. "Living honors the dead, Therion," Valdion said as he approached, his presence as steady and unyielding as the trees around them. "You carry their memory forward. That is the greatest tribute you can offer."

Therion turned to the elder elf, his expression conflicted. "They deserved more than this," he insisted, gesturing toward the flames. "A proper burial, a monument…"

Valdion's gaze was calm but firm. He gestured to the rising ashes, now glowing faintly as they spiraled upward. "This is their monument," he said. "The ashes rise to the veil, lighting their way to the goddess. This fire honors the lost and the found, Therion. It is our way."

Therion felt a warmth spread through his chest, a sense of solace he hadn't expected. His eyes stung as he finally allowed a tear to escape. Straightening his back, he saluted the fire, his voice steady as he swore, "On the honor of the Dracoseekers, the Arcane Vanguard, and the Emperor's Hand, I will bring justice to the false king. I will not falter."

As if in answer to his vow, the fire flared brightly, sending a single, radiant beacon into the sky. The light pierced the heavens before fading, leaving behind a sense of peace. Valdion inclined his head, a faint smile tugging at his lips. "Your message has been carried."

Rubelle's hand tightened around Therion's, grounding him in the moment. Valdion's gaze shifted to her. "And your daughter? Where is she?"

Rubelle gestured toward the modest hut nearby. "She's inside, asleep. She's been through so much."

Valdion nodded solemnly. "Come," he said. "The Council awaits. There is much to discuss."

Therion and Rubelle followed him through the winding forest paths, their steps quiet on the moss-covered ground. The air grew cooler as they approached the Council's glade, a natural amphitheater surrounded by ancient trees whose trunks twisted upward like cathedral spires. In the center stood the elders, their presence commanding and timeless.

The leader, an elf with silver hair braided with beads of crystal, stepped forward to greet them. His voice was resonant and kind as he said,

"Therion, Rubelle, your efforts have not gone unnoticed. To slay two of the ungodly hellspawns is no small feat. We owe you our gratitude."

Rubelle dipped her head respectfully. "The honor is ours," she said. "Though I wish we could have returned under better circumstances."

The elder nodded, his expression somber. "As do we all," he said, before gesturing toward a figure emerging from the shadows of the glade.

The woman who stepped forward was ancient, her form bent with age but radiating a palpable power. Her robes were adorned with countless trinkets, each one glinting with a faint, otherworldly light. She leaned heavily on a staff, muttering under her breath as she approached. Her eyes, milky with cataracts, seemed to pierce through the veil of time itself.

"This is Seer Serapha," the elder explained. "Before the events of the past week, she received a vision. She will share it with you now."

Serapha's voice was a low, rasping whisper that carried an unsettling weight. "I saw destruction," she began. "A kingdom in flames, its people scattered and broken. But amidst the darkness, a light… oh, such a light. The goddess's light, returning to restore the realm." Her tone shifted, awe creeping into her voice. "And this light comes because of you. You made it possible. You are chosen."

Therion stepped forward, his brow furrowed. "What does this have to do with my daughter?" he demanded.

Serapha's milky eyes turned toward him, unblinking. "She is Blessed," the seer said. "The goddess's blessing resides within her. Only she can stop the darkness."

Rubelle's voice trembled as she said, "She's just a child."

Serapha's voice was steady, carrying the weight of millennia, as she locked her gaze onto Therion and Rubelle. "She is the light," she said, her tone solemn, "but you… you are her sword and shield. Only together can you save the realm."

Therion's throat tightened. He had been in countless battles, faced death more times than he cared to remember, but never had he felt such crushing responsibility. His mind raced as he tried to comprehend the Elder's words. He glanced at Rubelle, hoping to find some reassurance, but her expression mirrored his own— a mixture of determination and quiet dread.

Breaking the silence, Therion finally spoke, his voice low and hesitant. "I'm just a knight," he began, shaking his head. "I've sworn my life to protect my family, to keep them safe no matter the cost. But this... this feels too great for us alone. We're just two people. How can we possibly carry the weight of the entire realm?"

Serapha's expression softened, and she stepped closer to him. Her ancient eyes, filled with both wisdom and sorrow, met his. "You're right, Therion," she said gently. "This task is greater than you. Greater than any one soul could bear. It is the fate of the realms combined, and it is a burden that no one should carry alone."

Therion's shoulders slumped slightly, the gravity of her words sinking in. "Then how?" he asked, his voice barely above a whisper. "How are we supposed to succeed where so many others have failed?"

The Elder placed a hand on his arm, her touch surprisingly warm. "The Tribes of Mythen will stand by you," she assured him. "You will not face this path unprepared, nor will you walk it alone. We will rally our strength, our knowledge, and our mythen to aid you. The light cannot shine without a shield to protect it, nor can it pierce the dark without a sword to wield it."

Rubelle's hands clenched into fists at her sides. Her jaw tightened, but when she finally spoke, her voice was steady. "You believe we're strong enough to do this?" she asked. "Even after everything we've lost?"

Serapha turned her gaze to Rubelle, her expression softening even further. "You are stronger than you know," she replied. "The trials you've endured have not broken you— they've forged you. The same fire that has threatened to consume you has tempered your spirit. Together, you and Therion can achieve what others could not."

Therion glanced at Rubelle again, noting the faint flicker of resolve that lit her eyes. He felt his own determination rekindle, a small ember against the overwhelming darkness. "And what of the Tribes?" he asked Serapha. "What can they offer us?"

Serapha straightened, her voice regaining its commanding tone. "The Tribes are many, and each has its strengths," she explained. "The Shamans will teach you to harness the flow of mythen, to bend it to your will in ways you cannot yet imagine. The Hunters will hone your reflexes, making you faster, sharper, and deadlier than ever before. And the Guardians will fortify your bodies and spirits, ensuring that you endure the trials to come."

Therion exhaled slowly, the enormity of the task still daunting but now laced with the faintest glimmer of hope. "We'll need every advantage we can get," he admitted. "This isn't just about us—it's about everyone who's counting on us. Everyone who's still out there."

Rubelle stepped closer to him, placing a hand on his shoulder. "We'll do this," she said firmly, meeting his gaze. "Not because we're ready, but because we have to."

Serapha nodded approvingly. "Then it begins," she said, her voice heavy with finality. "Prepare yourselves, for the path ahead will test you beyond anything you have faced before."

Therion and Rubelle exchanged one last glance, the weight of the Elder's promise settling fully in their hearts. Their family, their realm— everything they cherished— depended on them now.

***

Back at the Castle…

Oriana stood on her balcony, the night breeze tugging gently at her hair. Above her, the veil shimmered with an aurora of colors, cascading in ethereal waves. It was a sight that had always calmed her, but tonight, it carried a deeper significance. She placed a hand over her chest, where warmth radiated, a vibrant energy coursing through her veins. An energy the entire realm must have felt.

"Rubelle didn't fail me," she murmured to herself, her lips curling into a soft smile. "Praise be to the goddess."

The peace was shattered by the sharp crack of her chamber doors slamming open. The sound reverberated through the room, jolting her from her thoughts. She turned sharply, her expression hardening as Charon entered with heavy, purposeful strides.

"Charon," she said coolly, masking the flicker of unease in her eyes. "What an entrance. Did you forget how doors work? Or is this some royal decree about breaking them now?"

Charon's face was a mask of cold determination, his dark eyes fixed on her like a predator sizing up its prey. "You've felt it haven't you." She smirked, "The Goddess has not forsaken us."

"No matter. I will get the key eventually." He scoffed as she darted forward and grabbed his hand, forcing him to meet her gaze.

"But you don't need to." She plead, "It's not too late for you to turn around. Do the right thing… be my brother again—"

"Enough games, Oriana." He snapped shoving her to the ground. His heart trembled. She couldn't tell if she'd struck a chord. He was bitter that she could still spout such naïve dribble after everything he'd done. Turning ack now would mean admitting everything he'd done was pointless. No… he couldn't turn ack now— not even if he wanted to. Not with the Fallen Son already taken foothold on their realm. betraying such a malevolent deity would be the same as damning the realm to destruction himself. His resolve was made, he knew exactly what he had to do next. "I've come to put an end to this madness."

"What do you mean?" Oriana muttered as from behind him two knights stepped into view, their polished armor catching the faint glow of the room's lighting. Their presence was a silent but unmistakable threat. Oriana's faint smile faded. "What are you doing?" she asked sharply, her voice carrying an edge of disbelief.

Charon didn't flinch. "You've defied me for the last time. As of this moment, you are no longer a member of this family, this house, or this kingdom. You are banished, Oriana."

The words hit her like a physical blow, and for a moment, she simply stared at him, stunned. "You can't mean that," she whispered. "This is my home. My birthright."

"You forfeited that birthright the moment you turned against me," Charon snapped. "This isn't about you anymore. It's about saving the kingdom."

"Saving it?" Oriana's voice rose, her disbelief turning to anger. "You're not saving anything! You're blinded by power, Charon, and you can't see the destruction you're about to cause. The vision can be stopped— none of this is inevitable!"

His jaw tightened, but he didn't waver. "You don't understand what I've seen, Oriana. What I know. This is the only way to secure our future."

"The only way?" she shot back, stepping closer to him. "You're deluded if you think tyranny will save anyone. You've become everything you swore to destroy. You're not fit to be king, Charon. You're not even fit to be my brother."

For the first time, a flicker of emotion crossed his face, but it wasn't regret—it was resignation. "Perhaps you're right," he said quietly. "And maybe you're not fit to be the king's sister."

Oriana flinched as if struck.

Charon took a step closer, his voice low but cutting. "I tried to reason with you. I tried to make you see sense. But if you won't stand with me as I save this kingdom, then you'll watch it from the gutters."

Her breath caught in her throat, her heart pounding as his words sank in.

"Guards," Charon called sharply. "Take her away."

The knights advanced, their grips like iron as they seized her arms. Oriana thrashed against them, her movements frantic and wild. "You can't do this!" she screamed, her voice cracking with desperation. "This is my home, Charon! Where am I supposed to go?"

"You should've thought of that before you defied me," he said coldly, turning his back to her.

As they dragged her from the room, her cries echoed through the stone halls. "You'll regret this, Charon! You'll see! The goddess is watching!"

Charon didn't turn around. He stood motionless, staring at the balcony where she'd stood moments ago. The sound of her protests faded into silence, but the weight of his decision lingered, heavy and suffocating.

The silence of the room was oppressive, but it was soon broken by a low, guttural chuckle.

"A bold decision," a voice murmured, dripping with malice. "Can't kill her. So instead you send her away."

Charon's eyes flicked toward the shadow creeping along the corner of the room. It grew denser, darker, until it took on a semi-solid form. Two faintly glowing eyes appeared within the mass, and the air seemed to chill. "She has nothing to do with us." Charon growled.

"What do you want?" He then asked, his voice low but steady.

The shadow's laugh deepened. "Bad news, I'm afraid. The mage has escaped."

Charon's brow furrowed. "Escaped? How? I thought you said you had handled the oath-bound."

"I did," the shadow growled, a note of frustration in its voice. "But this one is… different. A special case, let's say."

"Where is the mage now?"

"Beyond the border of man," the shadow replied dismissively. "But that's the least of our concerns."

Charon's jaw tightened. "What could possibly be worse than that?"

The shadow seemed to writhe with a sinister energy. "They have a Blessed with them."

The words hung in the air like a dark omen. Charon's confusion was evident. "A Blessed? What is that?"

The shadow's eyes narrowed. "A Blessed is someone my mother... let's say, personally favors. She has bestowed a fragment of her power upon this individual. They are her counter to our little arrangement."

Charon's stomach churned. "Who is this Blessed?"

The shadow's answer was like a dagger. "It's the child of that Mage."

A cold sweat broke out on Charon's brow. "A child?" He recalled seeing the girl with his sister. Dalia was her name— 'But she was only nine…' He shook his head. "You mean to tell me a child is our biggest obstacle?"

The shadow's grin was palpable even without a mouth. "Children can be more troublesome than you think. Especially when they carry divine power."

Ironic words coming from the demi God that'd betrayed its mother. "But this also means she'd be easier to snuff out.

"What? No!" Charon shook his head, rattled by the suggestion. "I can't do that. I won't harm a child."

The shadow's smirk widened. "Not now, you won't. But once you receive your own blessing, your perspective may change."

Charon's gaze snapped to the shadow, alarm flaring in his eyes. "What do you mean by that?"

The shadow didn't respond immediately. Instead, it began to condense further, its form growing more solid. A low, guttural growl resonated from within as a creature began to emerge. Its features were grotesque, its presence suffocating. The hellspawn stepped forward, its glowing red eyes locking onto Charon.

Charon backed away instinctively, his heart pounding. "What is this? What are you doing?"

The shadow's voice was a whisper in his ear, cold and mocking. "Preparing you for what comes next. You made a deal, Charon. There's no turning back now. This is your **Curse** to bear."

Charon barely had time to react before the hellspawn lunged at him. Its claws raked across his chest, tearing through fabric and skin with ease. A raw scream erupted from his throat as the pain surged through his body, unlike anything he had ever known. He staggered back, clutching at the wounds as blood poured freely, but the beast was relentless. It leapt again, its sheer weight driving him to the floor with a sickening crack. His ribs gave way under the pressure, and the air was forced from his lungs in a strangled gasp.

The room became a blur of agony and terror. The hellspawn dragged him across the polished floor like a ragdoll, its claws rending flesh and splintering bone. His body twisted unnaturally, his limbs bending in ways they were never meant to. Every nerve screamed in protest, his consciousness flickering under the weight of the onslaught.

He tried to fight back, his hands scrabbling for anything— a weapon, a shard of broken glass, anything to defend himself— but his strength was failing. The beast's growls filled the chamber, a guttural, otherworldly sound that reverberated through his skull. With every swipe, every bite, it tore away another piece of him, reducing the once-proud figure of the king to little more than a shattered, bloodied husk.

Finally, it stopped, leaving him crumpled on the cold stone floor, barely clinging to life. His breaths came shallow and ragged, each one a struggle against the tide of darkness threatening to consume him. He could feel his heartbeat faltering, the cold touch of death creeping closer. And then he heard it— the voice.

"Your blood will be my blood."

Charon's head lolled to the side, his vision swimming as he saw the shadow looming over him.

The hellspawn, as if commanded, began to dissolve. Its grotesque form melted into a thick, black ooze that crept toward him, seeping into his wounds with an unholy hunger. The sensation was beyond revolting. It burned and slithered through his veins like molten tar, a living corruption that spread rapidly. His body convulsed violently as the shadow's chant continued.

"Your bone will be my bone."

The first snap was deafening. His broken ribs began to knit themselves back together, but the process was not merciful. It felt as though his very marrow was being scraped away and replaced with something alien, something stronger. His spine realigned with a sickening series of cracks, and he arched off the floor in agony. The ooze worked its way deeper, devouring his ruined organs and replacing them with dark, twisted replicas. His heart hammered with a new, unnatural rhythm, pumping the black ichor through his body as the transformation spread.

"You shall be reborn."

The pain was maddening, a crescendo of torment that pushed him to the brink of insanity. He screamed until his throat was raw, his voice echoing through the chamber as the final pieces of his body were consumed and reshaped. Flesh knitted together over jagged scars, muscle regenerated with a dark, inhuman strength. When it was done, silence fell over the room, broken only by his ragged breathing.

"As a King... as my tool."

Charon opened his eyes. The world seemed sharper, more vivid, yet cloaked in a sinister hue. He rose slowly, his movements deliberate, and turned to face the shattered mirror on the wall. What he saw made him recoil. His skin was ghostly pale, almost translucent, and his once-vivid eyes had turned an eerie amber, glowing faintly in the dim light. His hair, once dark and rich, was now streaked with gray, and his face bore the marks of his ordeal: scars that crisscrossed his flesh like a grotesque tapestry.

He clenched his hands, staring at the pale, claw-like fingers. Power thrummed through his veins, a dark and overwhelming force that threatened to consume what little humanity he had left. Rage boiled within him, and he struck the wall with a roar. The impact sent cracks spider webbing across the stone, the sheer force of the blow leaving the structure barely standing.

The door creaked open, and Aedric stepped inside, his face a mask of curiosity that quickly turned to horror. From his perspective, Charon was no longer human. The shadow, now standing independently beside him, had taken on a more solid form, its presence exuding a hellish malice. Its eyes gleamed like embers, and its jagged, amorphous shape seemed to writhe and twist in defiance of natural laws.

Aedric's knees buckled, and he instinctively bowed. "M-My lord," he stammered, his voice trembling. The air in the room was heavy, oppressive, and Charon's very presence radiated an aura of dominance that crushed any thought of defiance.

When Charon spoke, his voice was no longer his own. It was deeper, resonating like the roar of a lion, each word carrying an undeniable weight. "Ready an army," he commanded, his tone leaving no room for argument. "There is work to be done."

Aedric nodded quickly, his movements jerky and uncoordinated as he backed out of the room. The door closed behind him with a resounding thud, leaving Charon alone once more. He turned back to the mirror, the shards scattered across the floor like the remnants of his former self. His reflection stared back at him, a monster in the guise of a man. He felt the darkness within him, coiled and waiting, feeding off his fears and desires. It whispered to him, promising power, promising victory, but at the cost of everything he had once held dear.

His gaze fell to the crown lying amidst the broken glass. It had fallen during his struggle, a symbol of the man he used to be. Slowly, he bent down and picked it up, the metal cold against his skin. He placed it on his head, the weight of it feeling heavier than ever before.

The voices of the shadow echoed through the chamber, a haunting chant that filled the air with a sinister resonance. "Hail Charon, the one true King of Orivera."

Charon stood tall, his monstrous reflection staring back at him. He was no longer the man he once was. He was something else entirely, a being forged in darkness, bound to a fate he could no longer escape. And as he turned away from the mirror, the crown gleaming on his head, the only thing he felt other than a constant maddening pain was relief. That his sister was not here to see the monster he'd become.

***

Loyalty is a virtue—

A rare and steadfast quality that the Knights of Orivera all embody. The kind that doesn't just die overnight. A virtue King Charon had trampled over shamelessly. The Knights of Orivera had sworn their lives to the Monarchs, vowing to protect their kingdom until their dying breath. Yet, when the moment came to prove that loyalty, they had been utterly powerless. Aedric could still feel the shame burning in his chest as he knelt before the throne, his head bowed, not out of reverence, but by some otherworldly compulsion. His body obeyed the tyrant's command while his heart screamed defiance. He had sworn loyalty to the crown— not to the murderer who now wore it.

The memory haunted him, a stain that would never wash clean.

To think that he now served as Charon's right hand twisted the blade of guilt even deeper. Every time he stood beside the self-proclaimed king, issuing orders in his name, he felt the weight of betrayal on his shoulders. Yet, here he was, leaving an audience with the tyrant under the guise of fulfilling another of Charon's commands.

Sir Aedric's steps echoed faintly in the vast, near-deserted halls of the castle. The cold stone walls, once adorned with banners of the old monarchy, now stood bare, stripped of their history. The warmth that had once defined this place was gone, replaced by a suffocating chill that seeped into his bones. Charon hardly ever left the throne room, cocooned in his false sense of power. He wouldn't notice if Aedric's path diverged. And diverge it did.

Instead of heading toward the task he'd been assigned, Aedric descended the spiral staircase leading to the dungeons. The air grew heavier with each step, thick with the scent of damp stone and lingering whispers of despair. Torchlight flickered along the narrow walls, casting restless shadows that danced in his peripheral vision. He reached the bottom and approached a heavy oak door reinforced with iron bands. He knocked three times in quick succession, then twice more after a pause.

A tense moment passed before a muffled voice came from the other side. "Were you followed?"

"No," Aedric replied, his voice steady. "I was careful."

After a brief hesitation, the sound of a bolt sliding back preceded the door creaking open just enough for a pair of sharp eyes to peek out. Satisfied, the figure opened it fully, revealing a small group of knights gathered inside. They wore simple armor, their sigils scratched away to avoid detection. And among them stood Oriana.

Aedric bowed his head. "Princess."

"Don't call me that," Oriana snapped, her tone sharper than the blade at her side. Her piercing gaze softened slightly, though, as she added, "I'm no princess anymore." To Oriana royalty was more than just a title, and she'd done nothing but fumble from one failure to another. In a sense her brother had done her a favor, but she wasn't going to give him the satisfaction of knowing so.

"Let's get this over with."

Aedric nodded, falling in step behind her as she led the group deeper into the dungeons. The air grew colder still, and the silence pressed down on them like a shroud. The flickering torches cast long shadows across the arched ceilings and stone pillars, lending the space an eerie, almost reverent atmosphere.

Finally, they entered a vast chamber that had once served as a royal tomb. Ornate carvings adorned the walls, depicting scenes of Orivera's storied history. Pillars of marble rose to meet the vaulted ceiling, their surfaces inscribed with prayers to the goddess. At the center of the chamber stood two caskets, each draped in what remained of the royal banners. The faded fabric bore the sigil of the old monarchy: a golden sun rising over a silver horizon.

Aedric's breath hitched as he took in the sight.

The crude caskets were rough-hewn wood, hastily assembled, adorned with simple carvings— a humble farewell unworthy of their royal legacy. Guilt clawed at his chest, a relentless reminder of his failure. He didn't deserve to be here, to stand in the presence of those he had failed to protect, none of them did— but as he noticed Oriana fidgeting he was reminded that he'd come here for her and not himself. There was nowhere else he would rather be.

Oriana approached the caskets, her expression unreadable. She reached for the ceremonial dagger at her side, its hilt inlaid with opal that caught the dim light. She held it in her hands, her fingers tightening around the blade as if drawing strength from it.

"Charon may have thrown me out," she said, her voice low but steady. "But he had the audacity to release this to me. A handsome down payment for my silence." Her lips curled into a bitter smile. She knew he could have just killed her and be done with it, but he didn't. "His actions contradict his words, as always. But I'm done trying to make sense of him. All I want now is to lay our parents to rest."

Aedric watched as Oriana began to chant, her voice carrying a somber melody that echoed through the chamber. The dagger's blade glowed faintly as a strong mythen shimmered about the room in response, and a dull green flame flickered into existence, hovering over the caskets. The light grew, casting an otherworldly glow across the room. The knights stood in solemn silence, their heads bowed.

As the flames settled on their late monarchs, gently starting to consume the bodies within the caskets, Oriana spoke again, her words measured and deliberate. "Mother, Father. You were the heart of this kingdom. The light that guided us. Return now to the goddess's embrace, where no shadow can reach you."

Aedric's throat tightened. He felt the weight of the moment pressing down on him, the gravity of their loss. The other knights remained silent, their grief manifesting in bowed heads and clenched fists. But Aedric couldn't stay quiet. The words clawed their way out of him, demanding to be spoken.

"I… I wouldn't be here without the Monarchs," he began, his voice trembling. "Without Sir Galen. Without Uncle." He closed his eyes, inhaling shakily as the memories surfaced. "They showed me what it meant to serve, to protect, to stand for something greater than myself. And now… now I don't know who I am anymore."

He looked up, meeting Oriana's gaze. "I swear to you, I will do right by them. By you. I will find a way to make this right."

Oriana's eyes glistened, but she held his gaze. Slowly, she extended her hand to him, her grip firm and grounding. The knights around them fell to their knees, a silent vow of solidarity. Aedric followed suit, bowing his head as Oriana's voice broke through the silence once more.

"Return to the goddess's embrace, dear parents," she whispered, her voice cracking under the weight of her grief.

The flames reached their peak, consuming the bodies entirely. In their place, shimmering lights rose into the air, dancing like fireflies before fading into the ether. The chamber fell into a heavy silence, broken only by the distant sound of water dripping from the stone walls.

Aedric remained on his knees, his heart heavy but resolute. The guilt still lingered, but so did a newfound determination. He would not let their sacrifice be in vain. He would fight, even if it meant standing against the very man he now called king.

As the group began to disperse, Oriana placed a hand on Aedric's shoulder. "Thank you," she said softly.

Aedric looked up at her, his expression earnest. "For what?"

"For remembering them," she said, her voice barely above a whisper. "For not letting their memory fade."

He nodded, unable to find the words to respond. Together, they left the chamber, the weight of their shared loss binding them in a way that words never could. The path ahead was uncertain, but one thing was clear— their fight was far from over.

Epilogue

It was a grim night…

Therion stumbled forward, his body heavy and sluggish as though he had been running through molasses. The thick void he had emerged from clung to his skin like a suffocating shroud, and for a brief moment, he couldn't breathe. Then his foot hit solid ground, and he gasped, his lungs drawing in air heavy with ash and smoke.

He blinked, his vision swimming, and looked up to find himself in a clearing surrounded by flames. The Talian Settlement he'd come to know as a home was engulfed in chaos. Trees burned like towering pyres, their once-majestic forms cracking and groaning as they fell into smoldering ruin. The ground was littered with Talian bodies— their elegant forms twisted in death, their vibrant garments scorched and bloodied.

The acrid stench of charred flesh and wood filled his nostrils, and panic surged through him. "Rubelle! Dalia!" he cried, his voice breaking as he stumbled over the uneven ground. "Where are you?" His calls echoed unanswered through the inferno.

Then a shadow moved, flickering through the haze of smoke and fire.

Therion turned sharply, his hand instinctively going to the hilt of his sword. From the flames emerged a figure, limping but resolute. It was a knight, his armor battered and scorched, his face bloodied and smeared with soot. The man's eyes burned with something feral, something broken.

Therion squinted through the haze, his heart thundering. "Aedric?" he whispered, incredulous. "What are you doing here?"

The knight said nothing.

He staggered closer, his hand gripping a sword stained dark with blood. His lips curled into a snarl as he let out a guttural roar and charged.

Therion barely had time to react, drawing his blade to parry the ferocious strike. Sparks flew as steel met steel, the clash reverberating through the burning clearing. "Aedric, stop!" Therion shouted, dodging another swing. "It's me! What are you doing?"

But Aedric's only response was another savage attack. His movements were wild, almost animalistic, as though he were possessed by some unseen force. Therion parried blow after blow, his mind reeling. This wasn't the calm, steadfast knight he knew. This was a man consumed by rage, by despair.

"Aedric, listen to me!" Therion yelled, his voice desperate as he sidestepped a particularly brutal swing. "Where are Rubelle and Dalia? What happened here?"

Aedric let out a growl, his words barely intelligible through his snarling. "You did this!" he spat, his voice thick with venom. "You brought this upon them!"

The words hit Therion like a physical blow, his steps faltering. "What are you talking about?" he demanded, his grip on his sword tightening. "I don't understand!"

The Knight lunged again, but this time, Therion caught him off guard. With a swift maneuver, he disarmed the knight and drove his blade through his abdomen. Aedric gasped, his eyes wide with pain and fury as he sank to his knees, clutching at the sword. Therion knelt before him, his hands trembling as he gripped Aedric's shoulders. "Tell me," he pleaded, his voice breaking. "Where are they? Where are my wife and daughter?"

Aedric's lips twisted into a bitter smile, blood trickling from the corner of his mouth. "You don't even remember, do you?" he rasped. "You brought this upon us all. You… betrayed us."

Therion shook his head, tears streaming down his face. "No," he whispered. "No, that's not true."

Aedric's body went limp, his final breath escaping in a ragged sigh. Therion released him, his hands shaking as he stumbled to his feet. His gaze darted around the clearing, frantic, until it landed on a corner where the fire burned brightest.

And there, amidst the flames, he saw them.

His wife and daughter, locked in an eternal embrace, reduced to ash. Their forms were barely recognizable, their bodies consumed by the relentless inferno all around him. Therion's sword fell from his hand, clattering to the ground. He dropped to his knees, a guttural cry tearing from his throat as the weight of the scene crushed him. His hands clawed at the dirt, his chest heaving with sobs. "No," he choked out, his voice hoarse. "No, no, no…"

The world blurred around him, the flames and smoke melding into a surreal haze. And then, a voice pierced through the chaos, deep and mocking.

'A deal is a deal.'

The words reverberated in his skull, sending a jolt of terror through his body. He whipped his head around, searching for the source, but there was no one there. The voice laughed, a chilling sound that echoed through the clearing.

"You cannot escape what you have wrought," it taunted. "This is the price you pay."

Therion's vision swam, the flames growing brighter, hotter, until they consumed everything. He screamed, his voice blending with the crackling of the fire as darkness closed in around him…

Suddenly he jolted awake, his body drenched in sweat. His chest heaved as he gasped for air, his hands clutching at the sheets. The room was dark, save for the faint glow of moonlight filtering through the window.

Beside him, Rubelle stirred, her brow furrowing as she turned to him. "Therion?" she murmured sleepily. "What's wrong?"

He turned to her, his heart pounding as he took in her familiar features. Her soft brown eyes, her gentle smile. She was alive. She was here.

His gaze shifted to the other side of the bed, where Dalia lay curled up, her tiny form rising and falling with each peaceful breath. He reached out, his hand trembling as he brushed a strand of hair from her face.

It was just a dream. A nightmare.

But it had felt so real. The heat of the flames, the stench of death, the weight of the young knight's accusations. He could still feel the ash on his skin, the phantom echoes of that voice in his ears.

Rubelle sat up, concern etching her features as she placed a hand on his shoulder. "Therion, talk to me. What happened?"

He shook his head, unable to find the words. How could he explain the horrors he had seen? The terror that still gripped him?

Instead, he pulled her into his arms, holding her tightly as though afraid she might vanish. She stiffened in surprise before relaxing, wrapping her arms around him in return.

"It was just a dream," she whispered, her voice soothing. "You're safe. We're all safe."

Therion closed his eyes, willing himself to believe her. But as he held his wife and daughter close, the memory of that voice lingered, a haunting reminder of the darkness that had touched his soul.

Somewhere, deep in the recesses of his mind, he heard it again.

'A deal is a deal.'

<u>To Be Continued.</u>